Stephen Donald Huff's
DEMON WORM

CAPITAL IDEATIONS LLC

Published by Capital Ideations LLC
2733 Palermo Ct.
League City, TX 77573

© Saturday, August 1, 2020
First Edition Published 2020

Printed in the United States of America

Copyright © Stephen Donald Huff, 2020
First published in the United States of America by Capital Ideations LLC, 2020

All rights reserved. No part of this publication may be reproduced, stored in a retrieval system or transmitted, in any form or by any means, electronic, mechanical, photocopying, recording or otherwise, without prior permission of Stephen Donald Huff, PhD (Capital Ideations LLC)

Hardcover Edition
ISBN-13: 979-8352480458

Readers Rave About Stephen Donald Huff!

Must buy! (Terminus I - III [Conquest]: A Terminus Series Compendium)
"It was a great read! So good, I read it twice!"
--*Rebecca (May 25, 2019)*

A Helluva Lot of Fun! (Terminus)
"Terminus kept me guessing and thinking the entire time. It is not what I expected but, in the end, I really ended up enjoying it a LOT... worth noting is this is a post-apocalyptic book... Keep your mind open and prepare to be entertained."
--*Gregory D. Wehn (September 19, 2016)*

Strong Male Character and Strong Female Character Surviving Hell Because to Survive Means That Others Will Die! (Terminus)
"Terminus is a strange interesting story about the apocalypse. There a lot of twists and turns that will lead to area 51. I highly recommend this book and intend to read other books by this author. "
--*Modupe Hendricks (April 9, 2016)*

This Turned Out to Be a Surprisingly Fun Read! Chock Full of New Ideas! (Terminus)
"This turned out to be a surprisingly fun read chock full of new ideas. The world building is intriguing (mankind has been decimated by a signal that disinhibits our darkest tendencies) and the main characters are clearly complicated and - to some extent - less susceptible to this influence than are many others. I really enjoyed it. Nicely done!"
--*Tensai (September 11, 2016)*

Great (Terminus)
"A good story all round. Plot, action, originality, characters, and flow all get a big fat tick. How apocalyptic sci fi horror should be done."
--*Bean Bag (43176)*

Five Stars! (The Serpentine)
"Truly good read"
--*Steven Burget (April 22, 2016)*

A Twisty, Warp-Jumping Ride Through Space That Is Hellishly Fun! (The Serpentine)
"Huff's take on a fairly well-known genre is unique and fresh. I highly recommend this to fans of sci-fi and general probing into the human psyche when under duress. As I put it down it made me think about how one may react and survive in similar circumstances faced by the characters and reflect back upon how these situations still apply to life as it is now."
--*Gregory D. Wehn (November 14, 2016)*

Continues to Purl Amazing Storylines Time and Time Again! (Dark Matter)
"Some writers (another Stephen comes to mind) have an endless well of creativity and ideas for story after story after story. This reader doesn't know how this Stephen, Stephen Donald Huff, continues to purl amazing storylines time and time again. Since this writer is sure to not disappoint, one can only encourage such prolific bounty for many stories to come. Thank you, for showing us how it is done with such grace and ease!"
--*Amazon Customer (June 1, 2016)*

A Great Collection of Adult Stories! (Death Eidolons)
"Stephen Huff's writing is vivid and his stories are rich in conflict. The stories have a disturbing quality that sustained my interest from one to another. They leave a sort of "Outer Limits" impression. I hope to read more of his work. This book provided hours of reading enjoyment."
--*DataJanitor (June 9, 2016)*

Dark and Gritty Shorts! Good Reading! (Wee, Wicked Whispers)
"For those who like your comedy tragic and dark. Huff's writing is clever, intriguing, intense and every now and again gruesome. These Twilight Zonesque stories pick away at your mind. They are well written, often brutal, sometimes gory but a collection worth reading."
--*Allison Leinbach (June 8, 2013)*

Additional Titles from Stephen Donald Huff

Terminus Series

Lodestar (Terminus, Deep Origins I)

Simian's Gate
Simian's Walk
Simian's Way

Simian's Sin: A Compendium

Terminus
Terminus II (Control)
Terminus III (The Wild Bunch)

Terminus I – III (Conquest): A Compendium

Super B**ch

Serpentine Series

Watami
The Serpentine
Deadfall
Extremity

Astounding Bureaucratic Adventures Series

Corporate Lobotomies
Contractual Bloodsport
Military Milieus (Coming Soon)

**A Dog and His Man and a Chimp
(With a Machinegun)**

Bobo Machinegun
Perquisite Bombdog (Coming Soon)
Terrance Nutjob (Coming Soon)

Fiction Novels and Novellas

Havoc
Slate Gardens
A Cult of Fat Stanley (Novella)
Live-Jack (Novella)

A Tapestry of Twisted Threads in Folio

Of Heroes, None
Of Victors, Few
Of Losers, Legions
Of Conspirators, Four
Of Deviants, Five
Of Soldiers, Six
Of Monsters, Seven
Of Pranksters, Eight
Of Lovers, Nine
Of Plagues, Ten
Of Aliens, Eleven
Of Mysteries, Twelve
Of Rogues, Thirteen
Of Afflictions, Fourteen
Of Phantoms, Flights

Short Story Collections

Shores of Silver Seas
Wee, Wicked Whispers
Violence Redeeming
Death Eidolons
Dark Matter
Nightland

For the invasion – we are it.

Table of Contents

SEGMENT 1 1
SEGMENT 2 5
SEGMENT 3 13
SEGMENT 4 21
SEGMENT 5 29
SEGMENT 6 37
SEGMENT 7 45
SEGMENT 8 53
SEGMENT 9 59
SEGMENT 10 71
SEGMENT 11 81
SEGMENT 12 93
SEGMENT 13 101
SEGMENT 14 109
SEGMENT 15 123
SEGMENT 16 135
SEGMENT 17 145
SEGMENT 18 153
SEGMENT 19 161
SEGMENT 20 173
SEGMENT 21 181
SEGMENT 22 195
SEGMENT 23 205
SEGMENT 24 209
SEGMENT 25 229

SEGMENT 1

Thirty-one cats. All of them unnamed strays. Yesterday, she kept thirty-one cats.

Today, she counted thirty. One off.

Holding his nose against the aged stink of her, Bailey, the corner store proprietor, quipped, "Lost one, did you, Cass'?"

Cat Lady Cassie bunched her long, narrow nose to wrinkle slatted eyes colored verdant green, same as the lush swamp that surrounded her backwater village. Her skin paper-thin and varnished by endless decades of Southern Florida sunshine, the lines of her face flexed delicately over the angular bones of her cheeks and set, determined jaw, everything threatening to tear along the seams of years. Blonde hair faded to a tightly tied gray bun and everything sagging, Bailey thought she might have been a golden beauty back in the day. Before the cats and the craziness.

"How'd you know about that?" she squawked, her tone suspicious and paranoid. She squinted already slatted eyes simply to stress the point of her concern.

"Sam. He visited this morning."

"Sam? Sam who?"

Bailey sighed, this being a typical Cat Lady game. His own features rolling and round from all the soft, lazy brew-steeped nights he spent swatting 'skeeters on his front porch, the proprietor's voice stitched a lazy southern lilt to complain, "Sam Dell, Cas'. Your closest and only neighbor? You've lived down the lane from him for thirty years and more?" He portrayed his statements as questions, since this effect seemed to truncate the woman's dysfunction.

Waving his assertions away with a skeletal yet entirely capable left hand, Cat Lady next swept her humble purchases into a worn hemp rucksack, which she cinched tight to pull around her shoulders for her long walk home. Huffing, "Oh, that one. The man is a scoundrel and sex pervert. Many a time, he has molested me."

Bailey smiled painfully since he knew her remarks to be both true and untrue. Once, she and Sam had been an item. As he had said, thirty years and more back, when Cassie had first relocated to the Everglades from some frigid northern village of snow and ice. The whole affair had been quite the scandal – one that her first and only husband had not survived. Yet he suspected nobody had touched her that way since. He shuddered to ponder her cat-piss quarters. Thirty-one felines in one small hut!

Then he mentally corrected himself. Rather, thirty stood her most recent count.

As he watched her turn for the door, Bailey marveled at her stride. An intriguingly feminine sashay disguised beneath an old blouse and skirt combination, her gliding hips inspired slash-and-burn thoughts and an awkward stiffening of his attention. Despite her general condition, something about the woman still recalled boyish fantasies.

So, dark thoughts momentarily crossed his mind. He knew she lived alone, deep in the 'glades. Nobody around for miles. Nobody to visit. No family. No friends. Not one solitary soul to notice should something untoward transpire, way out there in the Great American Swamp.

Segment 1

All that, he marveled judiciously, rolling his eyes and releasing the pinch of his nose, *going to waste*. Shaking his rueful head, Bailey bowed to dip his right arm beneath the cashier's counter, where his soft, pudgy right hand fumbled for an aerosol can.

Rising again, he waved the resultant spray of deodorant back and forth through the toxic atmosphere lingering just beyond his countertop. With luck, he thought he might clear the air before the next customer arrived, since he knew they would sniffle indelicately to wonder what matter within his inventory had turned foul. Even Southern Florida peckerwoods maintained minimal personal standards of hygiene and decorum. Nobody enjoyed the acrid, glandular scent of cat-piss.

Nobody, he marveled, save Cat Lady Cassie and all lonely women like her. Turning his head to watch her traverse his ramshackle store's buckling blacktop apron, Bailey again imagined her small, lonely cabin festering beneath blued moonlight like a tormented scab etched into the greenery, and he wondered if she kept a large dog among all those cats....

Segment 1

SEGMENT 2

    Glancing backward over her knobby shoulder, Cassie checked to be certain nobody followed. She never bothered to ponder the perceived need for such security, but she felt compelled to ensure it, regardless. Anyway, everybody in town knew her and, of course, they knew where she lived, but this reality only argued the point since those who didn't, didn't.

    "Pissers," she gasped, pausing to hitch her rucksack higher and then pull a wadded red bandanna from the right pocket of her much-abused skirt. Tying this around her forehead and beneath the bun of her hairdo, she expected the dangle of its knot to wick perspiration from her forehead to keep its annoying trickles from her face. Glancing backward once more, she tipped her head to spit fiercely, hissing, "Between them and the goddamn government, only a fool falls asleep."

    Denim-blue. That's the way she remembered her 'Seventies-bound youth. Robert Redford and Paul Newman. The former known for his blue-jean style and the latter for his blue-jean eyes, and both being exceptionally rugged and handsome men.

    1977. That spring, just after her seventeenth birthday, she hitched down the east coast from Syracuse.

    Months she spent on the road, living from the same well patched rucksack that crossed her back now. Forty-five years, she silently mused, her thin lips pursed to a single, pink-gray line.

Bailey had missed the count by more than a decade. Then again, she knew time passed with a unique value in the middle of the Everglades.

Pressing sweat from her brows using the backs of her thumbs and a quick toss of either hand, Cassie started south again, this time bound along a narrow two-lane road that crossed a main thoroughfare before Bailey's store. Roughly managed and heavily weathered, this scarce band of pavement cut through sawgrass and palmettos to penetrate deeper into a daunting cypress forest bound in the general direction of her humble home.

Seven miles. Two hours.

Cass pondered the hike. From her left pocket, she extracted a rolled canvas hat with a lifelessly drooping bill that would surround her head with a halo of shade. This, she hooked over her hair-bun, seating it just above the rearmost loop of her faded bandana headband. Together, these two covers would keep her body cool and her eyes free of blinding perspiration and sunshine.

Measuring the morning's rising light as caught between the gap separating her hat's bill from an obscure horizon line, Cass judged the hour. Seven o'clock in the morning, give or take.

Inside another mile, that wide open wetland perspective would disappear behind a tangle of creepers, ferns and towering cypress trunks. Once more, the strange, swamp-bound passage of time would renew, and she would return to slowly, inexorably forgetting the wider country that existed outside the bounds of its insidious spell.

Even now, she considered how her understanding of the world had dwindled to a narrow, tenuous state, which encompassed Bailey's store and the softly sloshing 'glades that surrounded her bungalow. Nothing more.

In 'Seventy-Seven, American pride burned low, a pile of smoldering embers that marked the burnout remains of a failed war in Vietnam, Watergate, the establishment of OPEC and its resultant manufactured "oil crisis". Disillusionment reigned, while life spent within a college-town like Syracuse only reinforced economic divides and all such incurable social ills.

Wealthy students from the private university seemed to have every fine thing, while the institution's citizen-servants struggled. Observing these obvious differences early in life, Cassandra Lee Winchell knew she could not willfully suffer either condition. Though she would never join ranks with the elite, neither could she stoop to wash their feet. Plus, she absolutely loathed the cold and ice.

Even now, as she stomped along the pavement steeped in her own sweat, Cass lifted her aging head to admire Florida sunshine before cypress completely obscured it. Glaring amid its azure court filled with cloud-folk, that heavenly god stood over her like the promise of forever, smiling benevolently down upon her and all the green wonders of its kingdom keeps.

Once past the temporary dugout of Bailey's corner store and associated homestead, the tangled swamp leaned closer. A clinging, vibrant thing, its writhing arms of moss, vines and creepers encircled the road with an ever-clenching grip, as though welcoming her home again with all the intensity of a strangler's embrace.

Everywhere, life abounded. Death, too.

Her delicate ears traced raucous sounds of its eternal struggle. Countless things thrashed in eager nativity, ravenous satiety, sexual ecstasy, or terrified mortality. Day upon day and night after night, that sprawling beast both consumed and replenished itself, passing all through an infinity of gaping maws and pinching sphincters. Everything recycled and cannibalized everything else. All, a vast, stinking ball of rot and shit.

To be sure of her silent assertions, Cass breathed deeply through flared nostrils. Fungal spores and pollen. Bits of detritus, small as dust motes. Fragrant buds and flowers. Decay.

These, the scents of the Everglades, itself a sluggish river pouring sixty-miles wide from the low southern bank of vastly shallow Lake Okeechobee. Save for a few vital and most annoying details, this nameless spot had little changed since she had first arrived in '77.

Perhaps now she encountered more plastic in the trash that floated downstream, and she knew her canal-building government had hacked the swamp to bits during the interim, yet almost everything else remained the same. Then Cassie's brow bunched to reconsider.

Her eyes traced the disgusting goiters of a climbing fern, which had ratcheted its parasitic roots upward along the towering trunk of an ancient cypress tree. Allowing her vision to penetrate deeper into the sparse canopy of that moss-hung forest, she measured sloping sunbeams against towering columns standing amid ancient groves. Then she counted the boles that struggled within a green husk of fern fronds and invasive ivies.

As though pontificating her brooding thoughts, a flurry of movement to her right attracted her sweat-brimmed attention. Amid an overgrown ditch lining either side of the roadway, she watched a large snake slowly crush the life out of a giant rat-like creature. Both the Burmese python and the nutria had appeared in her beloved swamp only recently. She hoped the former choked on the latter, and good riddance to both.

Such foreign creatures thrived there. Cassie could not much care really, since she was, herself, an invasive species of sorts.

She had not originated within the 'glades, having alighted upon sluggishly reeking shores as a matter of slipstreams and random chance, much like the ancestral seeds and spores of all those lecherous creepers. Like them, she arrived to prosper and she had done so at the expense of the land's native inhabitants.

Kicking small stones from the waffle of her worn hiking boots, Cass squinted into the future as foretold by that seemingly endless gash of two-lane asphalt. She walked, and she remembered.

In the spring of her seventeenth year, having set the powdered sugar beaches of Miami as her goal, a young and most alluring Cassandra Lee Winchell drifted onto a strong and aberrant draft by the name of Lonnie "Lon" Seminole. Driving a battered Ford pickup bare-chested with a tepid can of Pabst sweating between his thighs, the big man had stopped for her at the junction of 441 and 27, where sweltered a crossroad town named South Bay. Its crazed borders collared the southernmost tip of Lake Okeechobee the way a bauble hangs from the neck of a jaded woman.

Turning her head slightly against moist, lazy swamp's breath, Cass peered into June 1977 with a squinted, suspicious eye. Neither sullen nor bitter. Never sweet either. Just suspicious.

Why should any man stop for a stranger on the side of a road in the middle of a small, forgotten village? Would the same man stop for a fellow? If he did so, would he stop for the same reasons?

Segment 2

Even the naïve, young Cass knew what men wanted. All day. Every day. Nighttime, too, of course.

She could naturally use her Scandinavian figure and green eyes with devastating effect. Yet her brief experience as a runaway had so far taught her the dangers of bait, too, since every helpless morsel writhed a barb and hook. Sometimes, she parsed that relationship with much difficulty, since fisherman, bait and fish all seemed to share a common greed.

So, she stood beside the rambling two-lane on the outskirts of South Bay, Florida, and she stared into Lon's wild, green eyes, even as he stared back into hers. She, presenting a ponderous frown and he a boundless grin.

Perhaps half a minute passed during this brief lifetime commune, while he said nothing, neither inviting nor dispelling her interests. Lon simply sat behind the wheel of his battered pickup, grinning like a fool and staring back at her as though he had confronted god. Or Satan.

Distracted by the rush of a passing sedan, Lon checked his mirrors and windshield for further indications of disturbance. Unseen for the overgrown horizon, he watched the sun die slow, bleeding light through a ragged lace of treetops. Cass remembered how she marveled to note the jet-black swatch of his hair pulled into a hip curl that hung down the back of his neck.

Green eyes. Dark hair. Swarthy features.

Her eyes strayed south, and she stepped forward to accommodate her interests, so she could measure his form down to the seam where his trim, muscular waist tucked into a pair of faded denims. Long, powerful legs thrust forward onto the truck's firewall to work its muddy pedals, and she quickly anticipated the origins of the man's nickname.

Segment 2

Corded and thickly-veined arms pressed large, neatly-kept hands to the truck's cracked steering wheel and three-speed manual shifter. The latter grip rolled seductively around the stick's bulbous knob.

Cass licked parched lips. Sundown loomed, and she had not found shelter for the night.

The stranger understood this much about her condition. She knew he saw opportunity in vulnerability when he stopped for her.

She also knew he could not see that mirror's reflection, since she saw the same thing in him. Again, she wondered what sort of man would stop for a woman walking along a deserted roadway that marked the middle of nowhere, Florida.

So, on first sight that fateful evening, Lon had quickly marked her for bait. Yet for all his native wiles, Cass suspected he had never seen past her hook to the fisherman beyond.

After all, the opposite consideration must also be true. What kind of woman would be there in the first place?

Segment 2

Segment 2

SEGMENT 3

By the time she turned off the blacktop to follow a narrow, rutted trail toward her sagging front porch, the sun had climbed high enough to stare down onto the top of her head through sprawling cypress crowns. Rising heat forced a rasping tongue across cracked lips, yet she paused there at the side of the two-lane, where she dipped the shade of her hat's brim to peer further south along its dividing white line.

Initially, she believed a large cypress limb had fallen across the road. Then she reassessed the lie of the thing, and she recognized it as too long and too uniform of shape and circumference to match her first guess. When it moved, she recognized its true condition.

Her eyes popped. Cass knew they grew large.

She had seen some big ones during the last decade or so, but she had never seen an animal like that. Two distinct lumps protruded from the monster's sleek form, each rising a foot or so apart perhaps three feet aft of the serpent's massive head. Six feet further along, she noted the presence of another large bulge and maybe several other smaller protrusions diminishing in presence as the beast's body tapered toward its thick tail. Its head lay upon the steaming pavement to lead the sinuous twists of its massive body.

Behind her, she heard the screech and slam of a rusting screen door. A shout followed shortly.

"Cass? That you?"

"Who else would it be, Sam?" she returned with a sarcastic drawl. Although he had stopped pestering her years ago, he sometimes intruded to offer rides to Bailey's store, among other amenities that she invariably refused.

Sam's time had passed decades earlier. On the day of Lon's death, as coincidence would develop. She had refused to know another man since.

After passage of so much fruitless neglect, her neighbor's hope reminded Cass of a stray dog thrown a scrap once upon a time. By now, she expected the flavor of his memory to savor more sweetly than any true act or emotion that might have passed between them, now so long ago.

"Some lusts rage like tempests and some like wildfires," she murmured. Both leave shattered, burned-out remnants ravaged and unable to endure further abuse for a long time after.

If this ideal proved true, then Cass thought her dubious relationship with Sam Dell had gone off like a massive bomb. Its explosive disappearance left nothing standing. Nobody had survived.

True enough, the two of them lingered within its aftermath, tottering ruins awaiting an inevitable topple and fall. Though they continued to be alive, neither lived.

Not for conscience or its lack. Not for remorse.

Rather, for something else. Something worse.

"What's that you got there, Cass?" called the old man.

Without turning her head, she traced his stump-and-waddle across the bowed floorboards of his porch and down its steps, then onto a graveled walk overrun by weeds and wildflowers. His property retreated only briefly from the roadway to crouch at the terminus of a rutted drive, which joined the blacktop across the same trail that she should follow toward her own home.

Shucking her burden higher on her back and rolling her shoulders beneath its weight, she silently cursed the man for a fool and a loudmouth. Like most females having advanced beyond grade school, Cass knew the value of a secret kept. Or not. Sam wanted everyone to know.

Crunching along the stony substrate of his rural drive, Sam kicked an errant beer can into a bar-ditch just before he stepped onto the two-lane, hoping to join her. In the same breeze, Cassie turned away to follow the side trail deeper into the 'glades, bound for water's edge where her humble home crouched amid mote-laden sunbeams and tangles of wild, growing things.

His once-stocky physique had degraded through time to a paunch molded between love handles and bad taste in attire, which today included shirtless overalls and rubber boots. Everything about his person appeared stained and filthy for lack of a keeping hand. His teeth crooked and some gone missing, Sam bared a lopsided smile to reveal all the deep cracks that lined the corners of his face. Graying hair grew corkscrewed and wild to match a crazed disposition, as the man managed himself with all the ham-fisted concern of a gourmand drunkard.

"Hey, Cass," he called softly, his tone etched by the familiar if twisted cut of forever-regret spun around infinite-longing, "why don't you call me when you need a ride into town?"

She could never understand the man's unending hurt. No matter how many times she spurned him, Sam continued to hope. He seemed to believe that her life centered around the pulse of his heart – or, more likely, the throb of his head. He presumed her eventual awakening to this obvious feature of reality, whereupon she must fall into his amorous embrace. Snorting, she tossed her hand to offer a rude gesture with her middle-finger.

     Sam failed to notice, because he skittered to a halt in the graveled shoulder of the roadway to squat, grunt and clap his hands excitedly. Having traced her previously enthralled stare along the roadway, his eyes shaded with an angled hand, the man hissed, "Hot damn! It's the same one!"

     Despite self-inflicted determination, Cass could not resist the anarchic allure of Sam's sudden disregard. Drawn by the nature of his tone, she paused to turn and take note of his display, expecting to find him where she had left him.

     Instead, she briefly caught sight of his fleeing back before he bolted up his porch steps and back into his house. A minute later, he reemerged with a pistol, shouting, "That's the sumbitch that swallowed Jenny!"

     Cass pulled her graying head backward as though slapped. "Your dog, Jenny?" As she spoke, she realized she had not endured the old hound's harassing bay during her outbound passage. Then she revised her first impression of the animal stretched across the roadway, assigning new concern to that bulge just behind its large, flat skull.

     Turning to confirm her dread, Cass found the animal all but disappeared, only three feet of its fat, stubby tail remained. Gone were the sinister head and lump-filled stalk of the beast.

     By the time Sam returned to the roadway, his pistol anticipated a vanishing target. *POP! POP! POP! POP!*

     Of four rounds, Cass thought the last might have clipped the monster's ass-end, but she scoffed at the man's

Segment 3

claims of mortal damage. She thought the snake would live another day.

Admiring her aged neighbor's distress, she skeptically confronted him. "Jenny was a big dog, Sam, and mean, too. No way a little grass snake could gulp her down."

Waving the pistol toward its absent intention, he replied, "You saw that mother! It was huge, man! Thirty feet, I bet! Maybe bigger!"

Cass waved her right hand before she used a thumb to squeegee perspiration from her brow. With the sun rose the heat, so she cursed and reveled in it, both. Observing slow recovery of roadside vegetation where the animal's warping body had parted its tangles, she estimated its girth, and she knew her former lover must be right.

Still, she perversely disavowed every truth that he uttered, while embracing all his lies as gospel. She grunted, "You're excited, so you misjudged. I saw a water snake. Nothing more."

Sam's eyes bulged. Now he angled his pistol skyward, waggling it back and forth to signify his frustration and disgust.

"A-, a water snake?" he stammered, indignant. To pontificate, he abruptly lowered his handgun to fire two more shots into the oblivious swamp. *POP! POP!* "Yeah! A great, big one! The biggest you ever saw, and you know it!"

Pursing her lips, Cass cinched her rucksack tighter around her shoulders, and then she pulled low the brim of her hat. The toes of her boots pointed toward home. "If you keep jerking that trigger, you'll call attention from the law. We know how that turns out for you."

That corked his bottle. Sam stiffened.

Straightening beneath the collapse of his brooding brow, Sam tucked his revolver into his right front pocket. His now unoccupied right hand moved over the scruffy gray forest of his bare chest, while his left shifted the swell of his aging paunch.

Five years, she had cost him. Cass recognized the accusation and resentment of it burning within his suddenly hostile glare.

A narrow smirk crossed her lips as she delayed her departure to take advantage of the moment. Any opportunity to torment him. He sputtered unintelligibly the way a lovesick man will do when a woman like Cat Lady Cass takes him into her paws, all fangs and claws and heartless curiosity.

"You don't have to talk that way, Cass," he ultimately gasped, his tone a rewarding mix of whine, injury and rage. "I never said nothin'... I never told them anything about... you."

Her eyes narrowed. Her lips pressed tighter.

She huffed wickedly, "I bet you wish that you had."

Sam's face fell. His shoulder slumped and he appeared to acknowledge his nakedness for the first time. The realization shrank him comically, so Cass must silently mock his lagging displays of manhood.

His tone broken and forsaken, he softly growled, "Lately, I wish a lot of things, Cass."

Smirk broadening into a passable rendition of feline desire, she replied, "Mostly, I bet you wish I would come sneaking along the dike some moonlit night to knock on your door and tug your bell-rope."

Licking pouted lips, he swallowed violent, lustful thoughts, but he nodded, too. "You know I would kill for it."

Segment 3

"I know you think you would, lover-boy," she angrily hissed, "but we both know better now. Don't we?"

While he fumed to make a response, she spun on her heel and quickly disappeared into the wilds of her home-bound drive. Cass need not look backward to know he would remain standing astride the center-stripe, his face burning and swollen, his mouth gaping and eyes bulging. For perhaps one full minute, she expected him to hate her.

Then she expected his demeanor to return to its unwavering course, his emotional compass aligned against Cassandra-poles and his faithful motor sputtering hopefully through overwhelming swells of a drowning fate. She could not twist his mind and body more viciously if she had applied a more physical style of torture. So long as he remained fixated upon her as his sick destination, Cat Lady Cass determined to pull his guts one slow inch after another, if only to cast his most vital parts into the briny deeps of time, chum to stir bottom feeders and worms.

Halfway home along that weedy trail, her thoughts at last deviated away from bad memories of the past to stir more recent bad memories sourced in the present. For a frightening moment, she allowed herself to objectively ponder the obvious size of that demon worm stretched so many times back and forth across the two-lane. Then she quickened her step, anticipating a need to count her kitties the moment she returned home.

Segment 3

SEGMENT 4

From the outside, her home appeared to be an abandoned and overgrown shack. Cass knew how everyone in the village thought about her. She had not missed the pinch of Bailey's nose.

"Shallow people," she grunted. Crossing the last stretch of her overgrown driveway toward her sagging porch, she mentally pondered the half-mile track leading to her front door and she tried to see herself and her home with the perception of an uninitiated outsider. She could guess how they might judge her, acknowledging her own low state by softly adding, "Shallow waters. Heads all packed with bottom-muck, so their channel-worn thoughts must run tepid-slow like an ooze of shit."

Same as the 'Glades. Steaming and reeking.

Her humble shelter occupied a void in the cypress forest, which locals called a 'holler', meaning 'hollow'. Beneath her tromping boots, the elevated drive to her front steps traced a curled ridge of semi-submerged limestone, which terminated in the rocky bulge that provided her home's foundation. Though it rose above the watermark by only a half-foot, its impenetrable underlying mass temporarily reduced the sprawl of green, growing things that might rise above it.

A fifty-yard circumference of sawgrass, fetterbush, wax myrtle, ferns and palmettos ringed her wrap-around porch, but the cypress could not grow tall there, so its submerged shield stunted the swamp's growth above it.

Lon's grandfather had taken advantage of this natural happenstance, reducing undergrowth to expand the hollow so it suited his needs. There, eighty years earlier he had built the house that sheltered her from the swamp's steaming damp. Passed from father to son to Lon and now Cat Lady Cass, she owned it free and clear according to the law and her husband's untimely death – all village rumors, gossip and innuendo aside.

Pausing at trail's end, Cass shouldered her rucksack onto the rusting hood of a forty-year-old Ford pickup. Given its perpetual state of mechanical rot, she reserved its usage for emergency needs only. Last summer, a plumbing matter had forced her to drive into town to fetch a new toilet, and the machine had scarcely made the return voyage.

Upon hearing the familiar thump of her heavy rucksack, a mob of purring, mewling felines came bounding out of shadowy undergrowth, alternately emerging from beneath the pier-and-beam foundation of her house, its riotous hedge, or from errant wilderness haunts. Contrary to the mistaken beliefs of scant neighbors and distant villagers, Cat Lady Cass never fed the strays and she never allowed them into her home.

If she stank of cat piss, according to the biased opinions of 'human beings' like Bailey Matchlock, then they could only be smelling their own prejudice. Of course, flaring her nostrils to make a confirmatory survey of a tepid breeze, Cass must ruefully acknowledge a pungent contribution from all the boxwood that grandpa had planted around his old homestead, intending its irrepressible growth to reduce encroachment into its crawlspace.

Lon told her the old man also believed the plant's particular odor kept vermin at bay, since it did, indeed, smelled of cat pee in the summer. Lifting her gaze while rummaging to the bottom of her ruck, Cass measured the lie of her clothesline, once more chiding herself to move it further away from the house if only to reduce foul ideations.

After passage of much sunshine and rain, the hedge had grown wildly. Fifteen feet thick and high, it surrounded the base of her porch like a defensive wall.

Maybe that same smell attracted the cats, but she thought all those swamp strays had simply found a safe, semi-dry place to sleep at night. Her home accidentally occupied the same location.

As she recalled when she had first arrived in '77, gators and wild boars had kept them at bay. Cats were scarcely a problem.

Lately, their numbers had exploded. Though she never fed them, neither could she bring herself to shoot or poison them as the locals advised her to do. Instead, Cass reduced the general nuisance of wildlife around her place by religiously composting the bulk of her organic garbage and burning the rest. The animals were getting no free rides from her.

Then again, her very presence in the swamp afforded them some small measure of service, since the alligators had long ago learned to avoid humankind wherever possible. This reduced presence of apical predators had no doubt turned her isolated 'holler' into a feline paradise.

Once her age-spotted hand settled on the objective of her hidden search, Cass seized a small, cellophane-wrapped box to extract it from the depths of her travel bag. Combined with a customary thump-gong of her rucksack landing atop the Ford's timeworn hood, sounds of crumpling and tearing cellophane called the last holdouts to make curling prowls between her mud-splattered boots.

Though she had long since memorized its contents, Cass read the label of the box as she peeled free its plastic-sealed contents. "One monthly chewable does it all," she quipped, "and healthy cats love them!"

Several of the bolder felines leapt atop the vehicle to molest her more directly. Knotted and kinked from countless late-night brawls, their tails whipped and waggled to befuddle her gaze. Lesser specimens lingered near her ankles, while the most paranoid and shy of the bunch crouched in the truck's weedy shade to fix her confounding likeness at the center of wary gazes.

Pushing the first medicated treat through the foil backing of its package, Cass delicately sniffed the thumb-sized munchie, this being a 'new and improved' flavor. 'Liver and lamb', claimed the label. "Smells like shit to me," she offered, extending one morsel to the nearest stray.

Being an aggressive Tomcat, it snatched the medicine from her fingers with a trace of fang. Hissing to drive it away, she smacked her lips to call the next patient forward, repeating the dose-and-hiss protocol until she cleared the truck's hood.

Next, she baited the ankle-purring variety and then, finally, she fixed the weird ones that preferred to hide in the shadows. None could resist the treat, so Cass must wonder what the company used to hook the animals that way. Heroin, she thought, or maybe cocaine.

Thirty-two, counted the label. When she finished punching through the foil, five tabs remained.

Cass smacked her lips to kiss the missing strays forward. So long as she kept the little beasts dosed this way – courtesy of Florida's Wildlife Commission – they

Demon Worm 25

remained sterile and largely parasite free, and she need not worry so much for her own well being. From month to month, she loathed to leave a single animal untreated.

Fifteen minutes, she circled the little hollow, calling into a waterlogged cypress swamp with kissy-lips. Besides the regular snarl-and-squeal of endlessly recycled life, nothing answered her beacon.

"Twenty-seven," she softly counted, returning at last to her front porch. "Four gone missing."

Not that she much cared, except Cass recalled the size of that massive reptile lying stretched across the distant two-lane. Mentally, she struggled to count the lumps apparent in its body, the bigger example representing Sam's dog, Jenny.

Apparently. If the man could be believed.

Why not? Making a final visual survey of the swamp, Cass stumped from one corner of her porch to the next, her rucksack dangling from a clenched fist the way a dead rabbit hangs from a hunter's belt. Though she had never seen one take a top predator, Cass thought they very well could do, given a rapacious hunger.

Lately, they had grown larger. Bolder.

"Another kind has arrived, perhaps," she mused at the last turn of her picket, where she leaned on a porch rail overlooking a riot of boxwood and a dense stand of bald cypress, her nostrils pinched for the stench of cat-piss shrubberies. "What do they call that sort? Something that starts with an 'a', I think."

Come to ponder the question a bit longer, Cass tried to remember the last time she had driven away a large crocodilian. Months, she guessed. Maybe since last year.

No wild pigs, either. No raccoons. No possums.

Something felt wrong, and she knew Sam had acted rationally, arming himself with a pistol. Moments like

Segment 4

these left her regretting an isolated, non-technological lifestyle.

Despite the drooping lines that hung with creepers along their gently descending arc from pole to house, her little home required no external connections to the wider world. Several years back, she had its roof covered with solar panels.

Requiring no telephone service – having nobody to call – and being uninterested in the so-called convenience of television or that worldwide-network-thingy, the humble addition of a small power source left her completely offline. Drinking water came from an electrically pumped well. With an occasional trip to Bailey's corner store and rarer trips to town, Cass had most everything she needed within a short walk of her front door.

Pulling this wide, she stepped into the mudroom of her front parlor, quickly pulling shut a rusting screen door behind her lest her home fill with mosquitos. Before she closed herself inside, she stooped to untie and shuck her boots. Then she carried her rucksack to her kitchen table, kicking her front door backwards into its frame as she departed.

Once inside and freed of her burden, Cass shucked her sweat-streaked clothing to carry it all in a bundle to her shower and a waiting laundry bin. Despite its outward appearances, she kept her home's interior spotlessly clean and tidy. Its sparse furnishings promised easy comfort, if so with a bit of wear.

Most importantly to her measurements, nothing inside the building had belonged to Lon or his dysfunctional family. All that, she had burned decades earlier. Afterward, like a small, grimy thing crawled into a dark, slimy space to sleep through a startling

Segment 4

metamorphosis, she had eventually emerged, golden and beautiful. Pristine of mind and body.

Pausing at the head of the home's central hallway, Cass secretly admired her only keepsake of the man. Small and innocuous, a splintered flaw that blended with the general defects of an aging interior, she knew one particular gouge between upper wall and crown molding to be more than a simple mistake of time and wear. Only a person privy to its origins could properly understand the nature of the thing.

A familiar smirk marred her lips. Even the experts had missed this clue for all its hiding in plain sight.

She never made any attempt at repair and for the same reason. After ignoring it all these long and lonely years, she had also embraced it. By now, that small, unobvious hole loomed larger than the volume of her purloined home, larger than the rare sunlit void of its nestling 'holler' and all its twisted family history, too. Some days, as she worked through chores or lounged through endless idle hours, that insignificant hole might be all she could see.

In it, an inky darkness that threatened to consume her sense of time. From it, everything bad.

Segment 4

Segment 4

SEGMENT 5

Crazy bitch. Confronting a standoff from the bottom of her porch steps, Belmar Dunkin determined to try again. "Look, lady, I'm only being nice. The law says I don't need your permission."

Cat Lady stood behind the rusted veil of her screen door to keep mosquitos and pesky strangers at bay. "Like hell you don't, kid! That drive is private property. You're trespassing."

Exasperated, the tall, knobby agent pushed a floppy campaign hat backward across his semi-balding head, wiping perspiration from his brow with the return of his hand. Sucking a deep breath, as per training, Belmar tried again, "That's what you told me last time, Missus Seminole-."

"Winchell! *Miss* Cassandra Lee Winchell!"

Belmar chewed his tongue. Once his enraged pulse dimmed, he continued, saying, "Miss Winchell, like I told you last time I came out here, I am a licensed-."

"You're licensed for shit!"

Now his head dropped in surrender. He had tried.

Then he remembered where he stood. In Southern Florida, Middle-of-Nowhere, Everglades. Casting around Cat Lady's overgrown homesite, a dozen mangy strays wended through his legs, and something struck a memorable note. In that moment, he had caught himself thinking about how easy it would be to shoot a man and then disappear him through the gullets of a half-dozen hungry alligators. His eyes bulged as his head filled with new and improving knowledge.

Like a key in a lock, the matter clicked into focus. Through squinted eyes, he renewed his interest in the notorious shadow that lingered just beyond the rusted shade of her doorway.

Retrieving his pack from the strap draped across his right shoulder, Belmar fumbled for his pad. Thumbing it hot, he punched at its face with deft fingers. Speaking to cover his work and without looking up, he stated his case one last time.

"As I told you before, I'm a licensed wildlife agent of Everglades National Park. After you sent me away last time, I went back to my office, and I verified your various claims of private property. If you care to see, I can show you how wrong you are." He knew she would refuse his outreach, but experience had taught him to persevere. Besides, this time he thought she might listen. "Your ancestors built this shack on federal property as part of a now defunct land management program, which expired before my grandpa died. Although park management tolerates your presence as a matter of compassionate concern, you have no claim of ownership here."

Now he held forth the face of his tablet to display a formal, legal document attesting to the truth of his assertions. When his host had ignored this display for perhaps one full minute, he flipped its contents to the next point in his argument.

"These are my online credentials. You can read my name here," he pointed to this information, "and this is my picture."

Segment 5

Returning the tablet to his pack, he next held forth a leather cardholder that dangled from his neck. "Here I am again in my official badge. Same name. Same face. Same job."

When she lingered without shooting or shouting, Belmar licked hopeful lips. He dared to lift one foot onto the lowest step of her porch.

"Like I said, I'm just trying to be nice. Call it a professional courtesy."

Cass growled, "You're trying not to get shot!"

Tipping his head to concede her most valid point, he acquiesced. "That, too, of course." Then, more coyly, he added, "You know it's a wonder the way a man's entire body can disappear in the 'Glades, should he have a firearm-related mishap. Hell, a mishap of any kind, really. Hair. Bones. Teeth. Everything turned to 'gator shit."

"That so?"

He nodded. He climbed another step.

"It sure pays to be extra careful, way out here," he added, his tone overflown with insinuation, "*Missus Seminole.*"

Her screen flew open with a raucous screech. Despite his better intentions, Belmar jumped.

"What's that you're saying, boy?"

The man frowned. Cass watched the painfully sharp bulge of his Adam's apple bob in his throat.

Recovering his demeanor, Belmar etched his lean, angular face with a mask of pleasantry. He shifted his hat to mop his brow, then he tucked thumbs into his belt the way a good southern man should do in such moments. Again, he sneaked another upward-bound step, so he now lingered only one flight below the level of her porch.

Grinning upward into her aged glare, his ember eyes sparkled meanly. "Look-a there... ain't you the one?"

Now Cass took her turn to squint suspiciously. When she stepped fully through the doorway to slam its screen against invading 'skeeters, Belmar's eyes bulged again to see a shotgun dangling from the crook of her right elbow.

"Ain't I the one, what?" she barked viciously.

Placating her anger with two upraised palms, the wildlife agent demurred. "Now, wait just a harebrained minute, woman. You have no need to arm yourself. What's the matter with you?"

"Like you said, mister. 'Gators."

She smirked, and for a mad moment Belmar saw a demon mocking him through the mask of herself. Before his better wisdom could manage his tongue, he marveled, "Lady, a devil squirms inside your skin."

Oddly, his remark struck no improvement in her hostile welcome, so he suspected she had heard the same thing many, many times through the last thirty years. Then again, he thought her silence might be worse. She made no effort to lower her shotgun either.

Finally, Cat Lady hacked the quietude by scoffing with a sullen huff. "Is that an official government opinion?"

Shaking his head to chide himself for a momentary loss of self-control, Belmar moved his cap around the bristles of his USMC-approved haircut. Deflecting his gaze to either side of the ramshackle home, he admired the swamp's closely kept boundaries. She lived in the middle of it all.

"I apologize for my missteps, ma'am," he conceded, tipping a shallow southern bow and then climbing that last step to her porch. Arriving there, he felt himself standing atop a gallows platform, and her the keeper of ropes. Then he wondered if he should press so far, only to scold himself

Segment 5

that he should do his duty. "Will you allow me to try again?"

"You little prick," she hissed, crossing her arms to prop her weapon across bent elbows, "just like that, you can flip your asshole-switch."

He grinned devilishly. "Can't you?"

Moment to moment, gaze against gaze, each measured the other. For the first time in many long years, Cass reassessed a first impression. Her heart caught painfully within her breast, perhaps hung on the impaling barb of a wicked thought or an evil memory. Through a flash of juxtaposition, she saw herself at seventeen awaiting destiny's call at a Southern Florida crossroads. There, her longtime tormentor invited from the cab of the same battered truck that she still kept parked beside her home today.

In the cleft of Belmar's dimples, the clean sweep of his immaculate teeth and all that bronze skin bristling light blonde, she caught sight of her former husband's lighter shade. Ever a cocky, arrogant ass, Lon had a way of making everyone who ever met him take a stand, one way or another. Most chose to dislike the man with a biting passion, while the few who grew to love him also did so with similarly violent obsession. Nobody ever met Lon Seminole to quickly forget him. Nobody.

"So," she grunted dismissively, "you have some kind of purple stink up your crack and now you think you're a hot squirt. That it?"

Belmar marveled. His grin swelled.

"I came to slay serpents, lady. That's all."

For some reason, this caught her attention. "Snakes, you say? What kind of snakes?"

"Big ones," he grinned. "Bad ones." He stepped nearer, face to face. "Scary ones."

Segment 5

Cass refused to retreat. Instead, she stood inside the aftershave reek of him, while sad, raveled strays twisted through their ankles. Defiantly, she stared upward at his chin, but she could not lift her eyes higher. Somehow, he knew her.

"Why should I care, if you killed every snake in this basin?"

Slyly, he returned, "You shouldn't. As I said before, I'm only practicing professional courtesy. In case you want to fire off a few rounds of your own, not knowing I might be working the area."

"As you say, a man could end up 'gator bait that way."

His grin matured into a full, open smile. "Exactly."

"Is that how you slay your serpents?" she asked, implying a reference to the pistol that he carried on his own belt. "You shoot them on sight?"

"Out here in the 'glades, Miss Winchell, I am god of my domain, so far as certain reptiles might be concerned. I can kill them in any number and by any means that I deem fit. Oh, and I don't need your permission to do so."

"Except for the fact that I might shoot you by mistake, which is why you visited in the first place."

Painfully, Belmar screwed his face into a mask of compromise, "That, and a phone call from your neighbor."

"He ain't my neighbor!"

As though he could see so far through the tangled swamp, Belmar cast a questioning glance over his shoulder. Of course, he understood the world differently, and he said so.

"I don't know the creep," she insisted.

"You don't need to know him for me to do my job." Tipping his head, he beamed a sparkling gaze down upon her, perhaps reading her mind like a badly written brochure advertising tours through a local asylum. "Just don't shoot at me for the next few days while I work this basin. No matter what you think you hear out there. Okay?"

She stood beneath him, unmoving. Silent.

Again, he prompted. "Okay, Miss Winchell?"

Without responding, she turned on a heel to snatch her screen door open and then shut again, returning to the shadow-bound threshold of her den. Staring back at him without speaking, they confronted one another as before, and he could not be certain of a passage in time.

Belmar chewed an anxious lip. He thought he should leave. He hesitated.

"Will you be back this way again?" she softly asked.

Once more, his grin broadened. He had that effect on women. Naturally, he nodded and tipped his hat, good-old-boy-style. Then he left.

He felt her eyes upon his back as he returned to his truck. Backing through the ferns and creepers overgrowing the long, wending drive to her place, he watched her front door and windows for indications.

"Oh, man," he gushed, shifting himself obscenely, "I got a thing for hot older women. Especially the bad ones."

When he saw a curtain flex, he knew. Next time he returned to visit Miss Cassandra Lee Winchell, Belmar expected the situation to get wet. Nasty wet.

Segment 5

Segment 5

SEGMENT 6

Cold beer. Fast cars. Hot women.

"That's the order these days, Jenny," he belched, lifting a warm can of suds to his lips without drinking, since he felt so thoughtful and introspective in the moment. "Used to be," he mumbled into the half-tipped can, "it went the other way around."

Resolutely maudlin, he finished his brew. He burped and tossed the can into a pile growing at the foot of his porch steps.

"Jen, honey! Fetch me 'nother!" he called stridently, slipping sideways in his folding chair, so he all but spilled onto his porch.

She could do it, too, his Jen-Jen. He had trained her right proper, but she was always such a smart dog. Fierce and loyal, too, just the way Samuel-no-middle-name-Dell liked both people and pets to be.

"So rare," he wept miserably, "like... like... finding a diamond in a pile of shit!" Groaning, he swept tears and sweat from his age-lined face, growling, "That's what this whole, entire world is without you, Jenny! Shit! Shit! And more shit!"

Pulling himself into a semblance of posture, he sat straighter in his chair to swat 'skeeters as he blubbered, "You were my best friend, girl. My only-est friend!"

"Who's talking back, you fool?" scolded Cass, having appeared at his back, surprise-like the way a coldhearted woman will sometimes do.

Sam jumped and turned to search slanted evening sunbeams with a blurry, alcohol-numbed gaze. "Who's that?" Winking one eye shut to fix a lone image among all the swirling facsimiles that disrupted his understanding, Sam recognized his most urgent evil. "Oh," he gushed, "it's just you, the devil. The real, actual devil."

Without asking or awaiting permission, Cass climbed onto the bowed and rotting boards of his porch. Absent a sense of pity and empathy, she pondered how Sam had let himself go since earning parole thirty-years earlier. Once he had paced five of a ten-year term, of course – which he claimed to have served for *her*. As ever, she witnessed the scrawl of that alleged debt written large across the accusatory backdrop of an endlessly hopeful gaze.

From one moment to another, she knew he longed to take her into his arms. This much, certain. Whether to embrace or crush her, she could not guess. This part excited her in a wicked way. Still.

"Am I your devil, Sam?" she querulously wondered aloud. Her finger traced the swirl of a creeper that had wended its choking length along one vertical brace of his porch awning. "And, if I am, what does that make you?"

For a time, his guts stewed a silent anger. He stared at her, his head wobbling loosely in the slippage of drink.

Screwing his eyes into a renewed and singular focus, he belched. He sat straighter. Noticing his nakedness, having for some reason prepared for this ritual, Sam recovered an old t-shirt draped across a small cooler resting at his side. Pulling this over his pasty body gone to seed, the man attempted something like dignity.

Segment 6

Instead, his gestures presented a wounded, hesitant sort of self-loathing. She need not hate him, promised the slump of his shoulders, since he would hate himself much, much more viciously and thoroughly.

"Thirty years or five," he grumbled unhappily, pulling a smoothing palm over his face and then pointing toward another folding chair leaned against his porch rail, "I can't decide which is longer."

"You never excelled at math," she tossed.

"It ain't the math, and you know it!"

He sulked while he watched his guest brush dog hair from the seat's canvass bottom. "It was Jenny's, you know. Now... now it's nobody's, I guess."

Though she had never much liked Jenny, Cass had admired the animal's fierce loyalty, always an uncommon thing. Before she could stop herself, she cracked real and said, "I'm sorry about Jen, Sam." Her voice too soft.

Then, unwilling to engage him in peaceable conversation, Cass determined to deliver her intended payload in a single lump. Sitting, her demeanor hardened, and she demanded to know, "Did you send that wildlife bounty hunter out to my place?"

Sam's face paled. He swallowed stiffly.

To mask discomfiture, he fetched another beer, only to pout comically upon realizing the permanency of his pal's continuing absence. Weeping softly, he sipped while confessing through the bubbles. "I worry."

"For me?"

"For the snakes!" he popped hotly.

When he started weeping openly, Cass leaned forward across her knees to pinch his lower thigh, waggling this flabby limb to attract his semi-sober attention. She held him this way until he accepted her intrusion by fixing wet, shimmering eyes on her demanding insistence.

"Finally, after all these years, Sam, listen to me," she prodded, shaking his leg more urgently. "Are you listening? Clearly?"

He nodded. His wet lips glistened sorrowfully.

"Yeah, Cass," he eventually answered, "I hear."

"Good, because I don't want to do this again," she asserted. "Piss off. Got it? Just leave me alone. I despise you. Can I be any clearer?"

Sam returned to sobbing unashamedly, his head bouncing and shoulders surging. Soft, snotty sounds issued forth from the lump of his curled upper torso.

"Thirty years!" he accused, his tone petulant and sloppy. "Since I got back, this is the first time you sit with me in *thirty years*, and... and... *this* is your message?"

"You had your chance," she hissed, stiffening to rise, "remember?"

"Wait!" he pleaded, extending a hand and stumbling to stand with her, only to collapse into his folding chair, unbalanced. "Cassandra, please. Please. Talk to me. One minute! You owe me that much after all I did for you!"

"You did nothing for me! That's why I hate you!"

He reached for her, but she snatched herself away, standing and wondering why she had confronted him after all these years. Why tonight? After countless vows to herself, all promising to do nothing of the kind!

"Cassandra, please! Don't say that!"

Childishly, she balled her fists and screeched, "*I hate you! I hate you! I hate you!*" Black-eyed rage filled the tenor of her harpy's voice.

Struggling against the effects of a twelve-pack, he again surged forward to stand and follow her off his porch, but she had not retreated. She only loomed over him, staring haughtily down at him the way Belmar had earlier stood over her. Sneering. Knowing.

Segment 6

Understanding his craving and using it. Twisting it. Maligning everything it represented, both of love and of lust. If her palm rested on the pommel of a heart-pulsing blade thrust into the man's chest, she would caress its handle and then slowly, savagely twist it the same way.

"To improve my hatred of you," she hissed, an incorrigible sadist, "when Agent Wonderboy comes back this way, I'll freely give him what you could never pay to possess! Oh, yes, he's already asked for it! I'll take him into my mouth and between my legs again and again and again, and all the while I'll be laughing at *you*, Sam Dell!" She cackled madly to pontificate, driving her point deeper, twisting her blade evermore wildly with each pressing inch. "We'll both laugh at you as we come and come and come!"

Roaring with rage and completely unhinged by the passage of thirty-five frustrating years, all of them crashing down upon his understanding the way a flood disgorges from the rupture of a high dam, Sam pulsed upward, arms outstretched. Fat, sweaty fingers clutched for her throat. She felt the brush of his nails beneath her chin, so she understood how narrowly she had escaped a strangling murder.

Despite his slovenly threat, Cass enjoyed great delight while provoking his unreasoning anger. Though this marked but one episode of many through the decades, she understood this must be the last. Unlike all previous disturbances, tonight she saw no evidence of recovery in the demented pinch of his hate-filled expression.

Like touching off a keg of black powder with an unexpected match, all his festering love for her had instantly converted to loathing. Tonight, he would murder her, and no regrets. No looking back and no fear of consequences.

Cass always expected their partnership to end this way – in bloodshed. Any day or night would do, so this moment would serve as well as any other.

Yet her instinct for self-preservation pinwheeled her arms to scramble her feet backward in a desperate retreat. Cass could scarcely breathe for laughing. Sam suffocated for spitting vile curses at her.

When she turned to dart across his porch, Sam spun to spring through his front door. Instantly, Cass knew where he was going and why. *He went to fetch his daddy's big-bore revolver.*

If he proved to be sufficiently sober, he would drop her before she reached the two-lane. If not....

Regardless of odds, she ran. Gambling. Once she heard his door slam open, she started counting her footsteps and his, too. Each represented a yard or so of distance, one fleeing and one chasing. How many strides would declare victory on either side of the divide?

Would she win? Should she care?

Now she heard his door rattle again. His heavy tread sounded across warped porch slats. Down the steps. Into the overgrown gravel of his walkway to his drive.

His first shot ripped through the air separating her right ear from her right shoulder. The second snapped through the bun of her hair – she felt a hot zip as it passed over the bulge of her forehead. These near misses only encouraged her laughter, so her torso collapsed over shucking thighs until she verged on skidding face-first along the swamp's muddy limestone floor.

Perhaps saving her life in the process, she hit the dirt on her knees to slide through her next footfall. Two more slugs ripped through the night where her head had been. Four attempts, she gargled, including three headshots that missed by mere inches.

Segment 6

"I should be dead by now," she giggled, stumbling to make her legs work again. She thought some people have all the luck. Most have none.

When Sam roared maniacally to watch her dart across the two-lane, Cass pondered Sam's bad luck and Lon's bad luck, too. Both, men. Both, losers. Both helplessly ensnared by the tangled hair that bristled atop her vulva.

One mucous membrane and two sets of lips. Endless hardship and misery.

As soon as she dropped off the blacktop and returned to the trailhead leading toward her homestead, two more shots punched the darkness. *POP! POP!* He missed from only feet away.

Six shots, she counted. The pistol's capacity.

Then, as she expected – or hoped – a seventh. Fired from an echoing distance. This one caught Sam in his torso. His lumbering form dropped instantly with a sharp, surprised grunt.

Segment 6

SEGMENT 7

Silently, she fumed. Caught on the return leg of her next monthly jaunt to Bailey's store, Cass stood astride the two-lane's center-stripe, glaring at Sam Dell.

In turn, from the shelter of his ramshackle porch, the man returned her enmity eyeball to eyeball. Despite the distance, she could easily mark a great, purple-on-black bruise that still covered his entire right torso, since he sat bare chested in the early morning steam, swatting 'skeeters with snaps of a rolled magazine.

Grinding angry teeth, she turned to stomp away home. A half-hour later, she rounded the last serpentine twist of the rutted trail to find Belmar's truck backed into place beside her house. The agent sat on her porch, apparently snoozing in her rocking chair.

Through slatted, complacent eyes, he watched her dose her kitties. Twenty-one treats, this time. Six more of her furry friends had gone missing since last count.

Before she mounted the high steps to her home, Cass turned a full circle to make a survey of the hollow. Insects in countless numbers flitted from one angle of sunshine to the next. Small birds darted this way and that. No alligators bulged the surface to stalk unwary prey, and the prey went missing, too.

For weeks now, she had noted an unsettling quiet. Belmar noticed the same.

From the short distance, he told her so. "She's gravid, you know," he concluded obtusely.

"Gravid?" Cass ground her teeth, given her silent resolve to ignore his presence. "What's that mean?"

"With eggs," he returned authoritatively, "but I think this one will give birth to live young. If she is what I think she is."

"Oh?" Cat Lady returned absently, enthralled by the swamp's jungle sprawl and its endless pursuit of both life and death. "And what is that?"

"One big mother." He returned jovially, motioning for her to join him.

That suspicious squint returned to her face, but she also dutifully collected her rucksack with its monthly bill of goods. This confrontation, she had long expected.

Indeed, only its delay had surprised her. To prompt its discharge, she climbed the steps, guttering, "I thought you cleared this area weeks ago."

Belmar grinned up at her without rising to greet her. Rather, he propped his booted feet more comfortably against her porch railing. Lacing fingers behind his head to push his hat low over his eyes, he said, "Put those things away, dear, and then come sit with me on the porch for a spell." Before his mocking gaze disappeared, he winked and added, "I've missed you."

Cass had used the tactic enough to recognize it when she felt it applied to herself. Leverage. Today, Belmar had it and she didn't.

After performing as instructed, she returned to the porch to join him, though he refused to relinquish the comfort of her customary seat. Instead, he pointed to a wooden stool, and there she sat to await his pleasure.

Naturally, Belmar stretched the silence as long as he liked. As befitted any sadist worth their while, he pleasured himself in her degradation and discomfort.

When she thought he might have actually dozed, the enigmatic agent announced, "He told me everything, you know."

Pursing her lips through an unseen shrug, Cass replied, "He always does, but I guess you thought you had some kind of magic touch with the feebs. That it?"

"Not me. Rather, you."

"Yeah," she snapped, "they call it a 'vagina'."

That familiar smirk returned to his lower face. Cass recognized herself in it.

"Cute." Now he sat forward, at last removing his feet from the rail to cross his legs, right over left. He placed his soft, floppy campaign hat onto the jutting toe of his right boot, which he waggled up and down before her own bent knees. His sparkling gaze mocked her. "Of course, I'd bet that you've always been the cute-kind. Am I right?"

She maintained her silence. He shrugged.

"Suit yourself, *Miss Winchell*," he purred, stressing the last bit with a trivial tongue. Once more, he settled into simply eyeballing her, but she felt it this time. Though she refused to fidget, he knew what he was doing. Eventually, he added, "You almost got me to do your dirty work for you. Almost."

Quicker than she liked, she retorted, "What 'dirty work' do you mean, Agent Dipshit?"

"Oh," he gasped, feigning injury, "that hurts. Ah, too bad. You're angry with me because I didn't shoot your boyfriend in cold blood that night. Well, I mean to say, I did shoot him, but not the way you expected."

Segment 7

Since she knew he knew, Cass would not insult his childish wisdom by lying. Anyway, she still harbored hope for the man's utility while Sam Dell remained alive.

So, she let go the rope in that tug-of-war staged in wits, and she rather drawled, "How do so-called 'rubber bullets' help you hunt giant snakes?"

"That was the unexpected part, I guess," he offered flippantly. Leaning into the conversation, he crossed elbows over knees to steeple fingers. He answered, "It's simple, really, and I would have happily told you so, had you asked."

"Had I asked, would you have volunteered to be in the same place at the same time with a rifle instead of a shotgun? That's what I thought."

"Chance taken. Opportunity lost. Chalk one for the good guys."

Now Cass took her turn to smirk. "Is that what you are, agent?"

Again, he shrugged, conceding the point. "No."

They stared at one another for a time. She could guess what he saw in her, but she knew what she saw in him. Continuing opportunity disguised as an arrogant gigolo. Deep inside, he would harbor deeply dysfunctional mommy-issues. This thought bared her teeth in a sinister smile.

"What do you see when you encounter a giant constrictor amid this Everglades paradise?"

She pursed her lips, though he seemed to require an answer. When he waxed stubborn, she prompted progress by replying, "A really big snake. Why? What do you see? Something horny, I bet."

He mimicked the purse of her lips. Then he replied, "I see ten pairs of high-end boots, maybe more. Two-grand per hide. For the really big ones. On a good day."

His logic clicked. "Rubber bullets do less damage."

He nodded through a wider smirk. "Indeed, but they're not rubber. Not really. These days, they're more like plastic beanbags. Oh, they hurt like hell, if that makes you feel any better."

"Screw you. It does."

"I expected as much," he replied, his tone void of judgment. Then his mood turned. He groaned to sit straighter, officially pulling his cap from his boot to plop its shading comfort down around his ears. "Of course, the same rounds that only put a cramper on a grown man's outlook are still lethal to the creepy-crawlies. This is why I'm here actually."

"Oh? Do tell."

"You have a problem, Miss Winchell," he stated directly, his tone honest and forthright – brutally so, "and it's about twenty-five feet long, probably a full yard in diameter. Four-hundred-plus pounds, she is, and ravenous. Why? Because a hundred younglings writhe inside her swollen belly, each one the miniature equivalent of its mother."

When she failed to appear shocked, Belmar knew. The way an entomologist will pin a fly to corkboard, he skewered her chest with the needle-like thrust of his right forefinger, uttering, "You've seen it before, haven't you?"

Her temper flared into a savage shrug. "How should I know what sort of wiener dog you're flogging from day to day?"

"Like I said. Cute."

"Look, what do you want from me Agent... what was your name? Belmar Dipstick?"

"Dunkin, ma'am," he stoically returned. "My name is Belmar Dunkin."

"Belmar. What do you want?"

Segment 7

Somewhat sheepishly despite his worldly demeanor, the wildlife agent returned, "I suspect you know that better than I do."

Returning to a course of honesty, she added, "Probably."

That self-satisfied smirk returned to his face. He asserted, "You saw me parked down the road that night."

She shrugged. "What if I did?"

"You knew I would be armed."

"So? Aren't all testicle-driven Neanderthals armed?"

"Sam told me how you provoked him."

"Did I? If I did, is that misdemeanor worthy of a death penalty?"

"No, I guess not," rejoined a ponderous Agent Dunkin, "but the rest of it might be. Like I said, the man told me everything." He winked again. *"Everything."*

Cass rolled her eyes. Standing, she dusted hands against her worn skirt, drying their slick sweat.

"He always does. You don't think you're the first, do you? Even if he did spill his guts... even if everything he said represents objective truth... what of it? The law has recorded that fool's so-called confessions a dozen times. He's always drunk. He always recants. They can never prove a thing he says, and I always deny every word of it."

"Naturally."

He stood to join her at her porch rail. Together, they admired the stifling presence of that primordial cypress forest. Death fascinated them. Life puzzled them.

Their elbows touched atop the twisted rail. An electric spark arced between them.

This prompted Cass to state the obvious. "Mommy didn't hug you enough."

Segment 7

"No," confessed a suddenly serious Agent Dunkin, "I suppose she didn't."

"Now you're forever in search of a woman like me, who can kiss it and make it all better." Something deep inside her body moistened to itch irresistibly.

"Maybe I thought as much the first time we met."

"Then?"

"Then? Then you set me up to murder your former lover. Thirty-five years after you set *him* up to murder your former husband."

"Is that what he told you?"

"That, and more."

"And? What's the rest of it?"

Belmar shrugged again. "He said he couldn't do it."

"You mean to say he didn't have the guts?"

He smirked. "Maybe a man needs more courage to resist the temptation of murder. Does that thought ever cross your mind?"

"Does it cross yours?"

Check and mate. He bit his tongue.

Switching tracks, he suggested, "Maybe I don't care. Maybe I still need that lonesome rub."

Her stomach rolled. History repeated itself, time and time again.

"Maybe the promised service might still be available. Maybe you only need to ask at the right time. In the right way."

Belmar pushed away from the railing. He fished a pair of sunglasses from the breast pocket of his shirt, fixing these to his ears with a debonair slide of his hand.

"Right," he acknowledged, "I'll keep that in mind." He started down her porch steps only to pause and stage a dramatic turn, adding, "Just remember. Nothing that passes between us changes your trouble."

"Oh? How so?"

"Earlier, I saw you counting kibble. Did you know that anacondas sometimes feed on adult jaguars, Miss Winchell? They do." Crossing her swampy 'lawn', he again paused dramatically in the gap of his open truck door. "A tabby would present no more than a mouthful to an animal like that. A woman of your slight presence might go down just as easily."

Offering him a middle-finger good-bye, she hissed, "It wouldn't be the first time I was eaten by a slimy tube!"

He chuckled wickedly. He waved and drove away.

Cass watched him leave while she pondered the young man's craven nature. Opportunity? Or threat?

The boldest of her twenty-something cats wended their way between her ankles, begging for love. Five fewer than her last count, all of them big, healthy animals.

Her wary gaze cruised the riotously overgrown dimensions of her homestead hollow. Cass shuddered.

"I really hate cats!"

SEGMENT 8

"Bitch." Sam complained in a low, subdued tone, lest some secret agent manage to record his confession. "I should have done it years ago."

Tonight, he had forsaken beer for whiskey, having decided to empower himself by getting shit-faced. "She's got it coming, Jen. You know that. I know that." He pulled long and hard from the mouth of his bottle, then he gasped, shaking from the foulness of everything. "She knows it, too, I bet. Maybe she knows better than anybody."

He drank again. "Sure, she does."

Then he cautioned himself not to drink too much too soon. Not that he worried for making a fatal mistake that might hang him in a court of law. He never hoped to live so long. Instead, he simply intended to finish the thing. Permanently. No screw-ups in the deed.

Afterward... why should he care what happened? That woman had claimed his soul decades earlier. Only his shell remained.

"I left this crappy burg a dozen times, didn't I, Jen? A dozen and one times, I returned. Always back to her. Ever for *her*."

Once more, he imbibed too deeply. He suffered the burn of it in his guts. He marveled through the resultant chemical thrill. *Yeah. That's the good stuff.*

Nothing but the best for a condemned man, he mused. Last wishes, and all that.

"Thirty years or five. Which was longer?" Since he could fashion no understanding of its utility, Sam spun the bottle's cap, hefted its meager weight in his palm, and then tossed it into the palmettos. "I know. I know all about it."

This time, he took a sedate sip. Like a gentleman.

He sighed contentedly. After tonight, all would be set straight. Peace would once more reign over Planet Samuel. Peace and justice. Delivered by his own hand. Nobody else would do it.

What would he say as he choked the life from her lungs? How would he act?

Angry? Vengeful? Spiteful? Happy or sad?

"Does it matter how a man kills his woman, Jen? Easy or hard? Fast or slow?" He swallowed air, fighting a vomitous urge. "Bloody or... not?"

His lower lip wavered. His lungs seized and his eyes watered. From the back of his head, he heard his father chiding him for a cry-baby. Real men don't weep and blubber and beg for mercy! Real men know how to manage a recalcitrant woman! Real men stick it to their enemies the hard way! No quarter! No lube!

"I came begging for it, didn't I? A thousand times, I demanded it, too." Another poisonous sip crossed the bitterest parts of his tongue. He winced. "Everyone in the village knows how I earned it! How I *deserve* it! More than any other!"

Passing a plastic hand over a rubber face, he refused to weep. He only allowed himself a single, protracted moan, followed by, "Christ, I wish I hadn't come back."

Too late. Too far. Too long.

Segment 8

"So many years," he groaned. "When did I grow old?" His mind's eye passed through the slideshow of his memories, all pictures in time focused on Cassandra's ripe, round ass. "Oh, she never ages, though. *Never.*"

A startling new thought addled his brain. He blinked. He wondered.

"She might be a thousand years old, Jen. Older, maybe." Sam placed the bottle's neck to his lips, but lowered it again without drinking, lost in ponder. "It's biblical, that's what. God and Jesus and all that. Come to call. Come to part the seas and make a sign in the heavens."

Lifting the bottle skyward, he cackled wildly, braying, "For thou art with me!"

Sure, he thought, god may be a bullet. Or a gun.

"When you combine 'vengeance is mine' and 'the lord works in mysterious ways', then what do you have, Jen? Hmm? You get the hand of god, that's what! Moving through the stink of things like... like... a demon worm!"

Now he drank hard. He drank deep.

For the first time in his dull life, everything seemed to make sense. Behind the bulge of drunken eyes, he watched that slinking beast ooze through an ancient garden to befuddle Eve and spoil the world.

From first moment to last. A sinful woman and the downfall of mankind. Every bad thing in a tiny, splintery hole. With a fast rewind through four decades, his memory machine returned him to a long-ago night and not far away.

In that moment, he stood in his best-friend's parlor, mouth agape and eyes bulging the same way, but for a stroke of fright rather than insight. The pistol had fired unexpectedly to pinch his startled face. His ears rang.

Blue-white smoke curled along the course of invisible evening drafts.

Lonnie lay at Sam's feet. Dead.

Behind the closed lids of horrified eyes, Sam relived his visual search of his friend's twitching corpse. He expected blood. Vast quantities of the stuff.

Yet only a trickle oozed from two small holes in Lon's neck. One in front, and the second in back, just where spine meets skull.

He recalled her boasts about the effects of such a wound. Laughing playfully, Cassandra had once claimed, "It's a hard stop, you know. No heartbeat. No gushers. Less to clean. That's the way to do it." Now he had proof of her grim assertions.

Her choice of pistols had also been carefully considered. A high velocity, small caliber bullet made small mess and noise, and she need not hunt for brass. All these lessons, she had attempted to teach him through a hundred torrid, lustful nights leading up to the murder.

Every minute, working him. Twisting his mind. Driving his desires. Every act pointed to that fateful moment and a single squeeze of one finger.

Standing over his dead friend, he confronted his ruthless lover, a mask of stunned-stupid fixed to his face. He recalled being unable to close his mouth or blink his eyes.

He could not forget the dangle of that pistol, its burning mouth breathing curls of smoke. Clearly, she could not forget his betrayal either.

Her gaze accused. The smoking pistol threatened.

Sam swallowed stiffly, then as now, and he remembered how an unspoken question had passed between them. Her query and his answer passed through unblinking eyes.

Segment 8

Cass knew Sam had not come to free her from imagined captivity. Instead, he had choked on his own conscience, deciding to confess his sins and then warn his friend of the danger.

Even after Sam's gut-wrenching admissions, Lon had refused to believe. The man blinded himself to his wife's infidelity. He rejected all consideration of her loathsome nature. He denied any implication of threat.

When Lon finally struck back in anger, he reached for his faithless old buddy. Not her. Never her.

Sam gladly took the beating. He offered no defense because he deserved none. No matter how he begged and pleaded, his condemnations and accusations of her had only served to further enrage Lon. The violence of his beating improved accordingly.

Over all, Cass stood, watching. Aloof. Cold. Her arms crossed. Hands hidden. Sam understood the implications of her pointed gaze. She expected him to fight back, to finish what she had started and complete his assigned task despite the initial misstep. Being so confident of his weakness, Sam recalled wondering how she had ever expected strength from him.

Of the two, Lon had always been the strong one. The leader. The one with ideas. Charm. Wit. Charisma. Luck. Everything that Sam Dell could never have.

Then again, he had her, too. This proved to be a poor choice. For both of them.

Maybe his jilted friend came to his senses in the end. Once he had exhausted his stamina, having pummeled Sam to the floor, Lon had turned to confront Cassandra at last. Same as before, she exchanged an entire conversation with her lover, every word of it spoken in the twinkle of maddened gazes.

Hoping to slip away in the resulting distraction, Sam dragged himself up their home's wall while carefully sidling toward its front door. Before he could escape, the first gunshot rattled his thoughts. Lon fell instantly at Sam's frozen feet.

    Sam stared at her. She, at he. Her pistol dangled.

Segment 8

SEGMENT 9

Nothing much remains afterward. Some hair. Hooves. Perhaps a claw or a few of the larger teeth. Almost no bone. Certainly, no flesh or sinew.

"Sometimes it takes weeks to digest a large meal. Months, for the really big ones."

"Is that right?" marveled Bailey, corner store proprietor. Blowing across his first morning cup of java, he tipped his chin toward Belmar's equipment belt. "You shoot 'em with that?"

Hefting his own mug in his left, the wildlife agent laid his right palm on the haft of his .45 caliber semi-automatic Smith and Wesson. "Only if they're wrapped around my neck or chest. Too much mess. Plus, folks get trigger happy out here when they hear someone else's pop-gun."

Bailey nodded. He sipped. "Yeah, I guess that's true enough. So, then, what do you use?"

"My hands, mostly," Belmar made a claw of his right fingers, snarling.

"Seriously?"

"Seriously," he replied into the face of his host's skepticism. This being a slow day – as all days tended to be in the middle of the 'Glades – Belmar sensed an invitation to talk, and he was always happy to educate locals about the threat posed by invasive species of all kinds. Especially pythons... and sometimes bigger species, too. "Those beasties aren't so easy to find, you know. They're ambush hunters, so they blend. Not so smart, really, but cunning the way ancient living things tend to be. Unchanged over millions of years of deep evolutionary history, they are so-called apical predators."

"I heard that term before." Bailey enjoyed another thoughtful sip. A judicious squint followed, formed the way all good southern men will countenance when 'shooting the bull'. "What's it mean, out here in the 'Glades?"

"It means only the alligators compete with them." Inspired, Belmar returned to a coffee pot steaming alongside the cashier station, where he added several packs of sugar and creamer to his brew. Stirring this mixture, he judiciously added, "Lately, based on what I'm seeing in this basin, not even the alligators are thriving."

"We were talking about all that just last night," informed Bailey, his eyes too wide and alert for so early in the morning, "everybody notices an unusual quiet lately."

"It's no wonder. Last week, I conducted an informal scat survey to c-."

"A what-survey?"

"Scat. You know, poop. Shit."

"You, what? You *count* the poops?"

Belmar grinned while blowing steam from his travel mug. "Everything – and every*body* – must defecate, Mister Bailey. Count the poops, you count the creatures that do the pooping."

"But... how do you know which turd belongs to which butthole?" Bailey laughed, and he had already begun fabricating a hundred different ways to tell this story to his customers as the day progressed.

Segment 9

"Oh, it's an art, I can attest to that. It's not an exact science, but the process is scientifically rigorous."

"And nasty."

"Truth is sometimes ugly. Unlike a lie."

"I suppose. So, you were saying that you went strolling through the basin counting turds and then...?"

Belmar shrugged cavalierly. He grinned, all teeth and bronzed youth. "Well, uh, long story short, you people have a problem, I think. A big problem."

"How big?"

"Maybe I'd better not say just yet," returned the wildlife agent, "since I haven't confirmed anything. No need to incite a panic. You understand."

"What can you tell me, then? What about the poop? Surely that can't be a big secret."

"No, not so much. Your customers have already noticed this part of the situation, apparently. It's the larger fauna. Of all kinds."

"Fauna? Another big-headed word."

"Animals. Like I said, you seem to be missing a host of deer, raccoons, possums and even feral cats."

Bailey scoffed by blowing a fart-noise across his lips. Then he upended his mug to drain its dregs, gasping, "I wouldn't say we're missing the cats, but deer? We all want to know about that bit, being mostly hunters of one sort or another." Waddling to the rear of his work area, the man rinsed his cup in a sink, speaking over his shoulder as he worked. "You say they get big enough to eat a full-grown doe? And they already just about ate *all* of them?" He shook his head to dry the cup with a wad of paper towels. "Then you go out there in the bush to catch them with your bare hands?"

"Like I was saying, a man has to find them first, and that's not so easy. For one thing, they blend. Second,

Segment 9

they're actually rather shy, and they can linger on the bottom without breathing for hour upon hour when spooked."

"So, what do you do?"

"Once I find a likely spot, I shuck my shoes and socks, and then I simply walk back and forth through the shallows, feeling around with my toes."

"With your toes?" brayed an amazed store proprietor. "Go on! You do not!"

"I do, I do! They try to play dumb when you step on them, but it only takes once and then a man never forgets the feel of a giant serpent beneath his feet. I've trod upon their heads without eliciting so much as a flinch from the bastards. Oh, they're cool hunters, alright, and they know they have no need to worry about the average footfall."

"Of course, yours ain't average. Right, King Kong?"

Grinning abashedly in a self-deprecating way that endeared the man to both genders, Belmar accepted the praise as well-deserved. "No, I suppose they ain't, Mister Bailey."

"Then what happens? A battle-royale?"

"Sometimes, when I'm working with a crew to wrangle a whopper, but the work is routine, day-to-day. Most times, it's easiest and fastest to get a grip on them immediately, but that takes three with a big one. At least. Maybe more, for the giants." Setting his travel mug aside, Belmar straddled the floor as though mounting a porker, his hands extended like claws to grapple the monster lying in wait between his ankles. "It's a huge mistake to take one of the big ones while flying solo. No matter where you grab it, the animal can encircle and crush its attacker. With at least three good people though, you get it by the head like this," he snatched his hands downward, clamping a tight grip on the serpent's invisible neck, "while someone gets the middle and someone else gets the tail at the same time. Then you just pull against one another as though playing tug-of-war. So long as the thing can't jerk itself into a curl, it remains manageable enough."

"And if it can?"

Belmar stood, dusting hands that he had not dirtied. He returned to his mug, sipping while shaking his head thoughtfully. "That's the fun part," he gushed happily, "your so-called 'battle royale'. Sometimes, it gets hairy, and you ain't felt a squeeze until you get a thirty-two-foot Burmese python curled once or twice around a body part."

"Does it hurt?"

"If a man doesn't do something to save himself, it can crush a muscle or break bones, maybe do permanent damage. No matter what, something like that reminds a man of so many forgotten ideations."

"Like what?"

"Like, we used to be dinner much more often than we are now. Lions and tigers and bears."

"Oh, my!" Bailey perched atop a tall stool situated behind the counter. "I know you're anxious to get to the hunt but take time to tell me about the biggest one you ever caught."

Cocking his head thoughtfully, Belmar leaned against the same counter, crossing one foot over another with a confident ease. "I think you want to hear about the scariest, since bigger is not always badder."

"No?"

The agent shook his head behind a broad grin. "So, I'll tell you about something that happened a couple of counties south of here. In the 'Glades, we mostly get pythons and boas, all of them descendants of castoff pets.

Now, several different species thrive here, but the Burmese variety is king. It gets to be a couple of hundred pounds at thirty-plus feet long. Maybe eight inches in diameter. That's about two feet around. Bigger than almost all other pythons and boas."

Bailey gauged the distance to his gas pumps, then extended his estimate all the way to the road, across both lanes. He whistled the way any good southern boy will do when properly impressed. "That's a mighty big snake!"

Tipping his head, Belmar conceded, "By length, the biggest. Not the baddest though, and not the heaviest. That award goes to something new in these parts."

"Yeah? What's that?"

"It's a boa. The king of all snakes." Rolling his lips and tongue to impress, the younger man drawled, "Anaconda," pronouncing each syllable with exacting clarity.

"Is that a big one?"

"Well, I know a couple different kinds of 'big'. The one I'm talking about now is a green anaconda. That kind is 'big-heavy'. I also happen to be talking about the reticulated python. That one is 'big-long', but it can also be 'big-heavy'."

"That so? How long? How heavy?"

"Thirty feet and more. A couple hundred pounds. The green – we call them 'porkers' – it can grow to four-hundred."

"Pounds?"

"Right. Of course, the anaconda is not a terribly long snake. Most barely stretch through twenty."

"Feet?"

"Right. That kind might get to be a foot in diameter – that's a full yard in circumference. All around, you know."

"Oh, I know about circumference."

"Right. The reticulated python, on the other hand, barely makes six or eight inches in diameter. Maybe a foot, all the way round."

Bailey whistled and rolled his eyes. Reaching for a magazine to fan himself for the morning's rising steam, he clucked his tongue. "That's one big mother!"

Laughing, Belmar agreed. He returned his mug to both palms, sipping.

"So, back to the story, I was working a basin two counties south of here-."

"Broward?"

"And west some, on the Collier side."

Again, Bailey rolled his eyes. He fanned. He groaned. "That figures. Everything is weirder on the Gulf-edge."

"We get calls from all over, these days. Miami, even. Some of the best neighborhoods, too. I've pulled them out of toilets, bathtubs, washing machines, swimming pools, clothes hampers, dresser drawers, cars of all shapes and sizes and – once – a male-oriented sexual device. No shit. Now this-."

"A what?" drawled Bailey, clearly disturbed.

"It's kind of a long tube with a suction pump on one end, and you apparently-."

"Not me!"

"Anyway, this particular call, I was working with two younger apprentices, both of them named 'Bob', no kidding. I call them Bob One and Bob Two."

"Funny."

"Yeah, so – long story short – I was showing them how to catch a big one, because they asked, being full of piss and vinegar the way young men will be."

"Don't I know it!"

"Oh, they had balls enough to do the job, I guess. Anyway, I managed to coax them into the water, which was just high enough to drag my sack."

"So, not too deep." They laughed.

"By then I had pretty well mapped out the lie of the animal – or so I thought – and I directed the bigger kid to get a grip on the monster's belly, while the smaller one would work the tail. Being senior, I got the head. What we do is, we get setup this way and then we all three plunge our hands into the water to just snatch the thing up."

"Sure enough? That's all it takes? Like noodling catfish!"

"Naturally, as soon as it feels itself rise out of the water, the snake wakes up – 'cause usually they're dozing – and then it starts acting stupid."

"How stupid?"

"Real stupid. Sometimes, stupid enough to crush a man to death or break a limb."

"Go on!"

"It happens a few times a year, but what makes this particular incident so interesting is what came up with the snatch. Head and tummy, both connected. Me and the heavier kid, we happened to get a hold of the same snake, this being a monster-sized reticulated python, one of the biggest I had ever seen."

"Uh-uh, and what'd the littler kid get? Something different, I bet!"

"Turns out, the smaller fellah latched onto the ass-end of a green anaconda! Not the biggest specimen in the bayou, but it was a fat one. During necropsy, we found it stuffed full of deer, having recently eaten a doe and two fawns."

"You don't say! Then what happened?"

"Well, this last bit is important, because the thing was so heavy and bloated, it could scarcely coil itself around the kid's legs. Of course, as soon as I saw not one but *two* giant heads lunging out of the soup, I knew we were all three in trouble. *Real* trouble."

"You pissed-off both without getting either of 'em in the bag!"

"You should have seen the smaller kid's face! I almost herniated myself laughing!" Belmar chuckled, then he sobered a bit to sip coffee and append, "All he had to do was just let the thing go. Only, the fact that he had caught hold of an entirely different snake didn't register with the boy, and he started doing exactly what I had told him to do."

"He started pulling backwards on it!"

"As fast as he could pedal through the muck! The more he backwatered, the higher that conda's head reared and the bigger the kid's eyes bulged! Meanwhile, having grabbed the middle part of half a python – so another fifteen feet of the monster remained loose – the bigger boy just froze."

Bailey shook his head as he fanned. "*Mmm-mmm-mmm.* That's never a good thing to do in a tight situation. In such times, a man has just got to clench his teeth, bunch his butt cheeks and get to work!"

"I have no room to talk, really, because I was laughing so hard that I forgot to let go the bigger snake, too, so I next watched it whip around Bob Two's legs and waist, with the last curl wrapping around his neck, quick as you like. If I thought Bob One had perfected the most astonishing 'oh-shit' face that I had ever seen, then Bob Two's expression broke the mold!"

"I bet!"

"'Cause about that time, my grip slipped and that python rose up, reared backward and then... *WHAP!*" Belmar made a snake of his right hand to attack himself, spilling coffee with the display. "It bit me. Directly on top of my head."

"Directly on top? Like a hat?"

"Right, like a snake-hat. Most people don't know that a big python has needle-like fangs maybe three inches long. More. All angled backwards into the throat, so they make a kind of one-way ratchet as the animal chews."

"And a man's head gushes when cut."

"Right," Belmar oozed, lifting his cap and tipping his balding crewcut to expose twin rows of parallel scars. Bailey ogled for a proper look before the agent straightened, laughing. "By the time Bob Two starts breathing again-."

"He's all balled-up!"

"And Bob One? He managed to climb back onto the roadbed, but he didn't bother to take the truck. No, sir. Instead, he lit out for home, running the entire way." Belmar slapped his empty hand atop his thigh, so his host jumped, startled. "I think he might have sprinted the entire seventy miles, but guess what? A pissed-off anaconda can really move! It's a helluva sight. I thought a little girl started screaming, but it might have been him or me."

"Or Bob Two!"

"Right. Of course, a three-hundred-pound python has a way of sobering a man's thoughts, too, especially when it's attached to his skull and double-specially after it twists a guy down into the muck and water, there to drown." Belmar paused to shudder properly, again shaking his head and sipping warm coffee.

"Dear lord." Bailey leaned forward, fanning himself faster. "What'd you do, man?"

Segment 9

Belmar winked and grinned. "I died, of course."

The older man's mouth dropped. His face fell.

"Well," disclaimed the abashed wildlife agent, "almost. Fortunately for me and Bob Two, the First Bob turned out to be a fast runner, because he ditched the 'conda about a mile down the trail. I thought he had quit and gone home, for sure, but he came back just in time to find his pal turning blue and trying to tap-out."

"You used the pistol."

Shaking his head, Belmar noted a glint of sunlight shining through the store's plate glass windows. He sidled toward the door. "Nope. I thought about it, of course," he made a pistol of his right thumb and forefinger, mimicking the required head shot, "but only a fool has that kind of confidence with a giant snake making a general mess of things."

When the younger man appeared ready to depart without finishing the story, Bailey dropped off his stool to lean over the counter. "Hey, now! You're not going to leave things hanging that way, are you? What happened to the snake?"

"Well, sir," drawled Belmar, pushing the door open wide, "a fellah always wants more, but – in a real pinch – three guys are just enough to do the job. Just. By now, I guess the scaly little guy is stomping around Coral Gables or Manhattan as a half-dozen pair of shoes. *Cha-ching!* See ya later, Mister Bailey!"

"I guess I'll get the rest next time!" Speaking after the closing door, Bailey huffed, "And it's Mister *Matchlock*, you crazy bastard." Then he plopped his rump atop the stool to continue fanning himself with resolute determination.

Segment 9

SEGMENT 10

"I know two different kinds of smart," humped Belmar, cinching his pack and shotgun higher to ease a pinch in his sweat-soaked shirt, "you got your book-smarts and then you got everything else."

The three men dragged their legs through the muck, mud and roots of the swamp's bottom, while chocolate-milk water swirled around their thighs just about their knees. Waddling their way along a submerged limestone ridge toward a promising shallow, they pinwheeled extended arms to aid their lumbering progress while holding their hands high above the drink.

"Both kinds have their value," he instructed his summer interns, Bob One and Bob Two, "but each kind gets paid a different way."

The bigger boy, Bob Two, wrung sweat from beneath the floppy bill of his campaign hat, drawling, "Which gets paid the most?"

An apt question, thought Belmar, so he acknowledged this truth by tipping his head and wringing sweat from beneath his own cap. "Both and neither. Pay doesn't depend on smarts, so much as it depends on will or desire."

"Or luck," from Bob One.

"Yep, luck helps, but luck don't mean much to a good man."

"A good man like you?"

Belmar shrugged humbly. "I was thinking of my daddy."

"Which kind was he?"

"He was a rare breed, I think, since he was of both kinds."

"Like you," repeated Bob One.

"Someday, maybe."

Impatient with his younger friend's interruption Bob Two prodded, "What about the pay is different, if not the amount?"

"Another good question," asserted the senior wildlife agent, extending his hand and lifting his sodden right boot to climb the mossy trunk of a fallen cypress. Grunting, he taught, "As far as I can tell, book-smarts pay like a commodity, since it represents something that a person owns, something to be sold or rented to the highest bidder. Universities work like brokers to dispense the license or credential or degree – whatever – that represents the value in question. You do time in a classroom, pass a few tests, then they give you a distributorship, of a kind."

Exhibiting much less grace and skill, the Bobs followed their mentor over the long, rounded wall of the cypress trunk, which lay at waist-height. Both kept their eyes focused forward to avoid thinking about all the slimy stuff they must touch. With their hands. Their *bare* hands!

On the far side, having much experience with such matters, Belmar had carefully selected his landing place. He knew leaping deer occasionally wallowed deep holes on either side of such crossings, so he descended hard right, finding firm ground atop a clump of sawgrass and sedge.

Bob Two landed nearby, soaked to his waist, yet managing to keep his upper torso dry. Behind him, Bob One struggled with a snarled loop of creeper. Freeing himself from it, he spun around atop the fallen bole, his feet dangling. Seeing his companions standing high and dry a few feet lower, he grinned and then dropped off the log.

Belmar watched the young man hit the murky water and then plunge to an unexpected depth. His cap floated on the surface, while his head disappeared beneath several more feet of shit-soup. The looming afterglow of his wide, surprised gaze lingered atop disturbed ripples.

Then he burst from the surface, gasping and choking. His mouth overflowed with the earthy liquid. Watergrass hung from his ears.

"Hot damn!" he gasped, shuddering and sputtering while attempting to rise and walk on water like the savior. "Hot damn!"

Bob Two tried to help, but his outstretched grip faltered when his body curled over with laughter. Belmar made no attempt at all since he also could not breathe for laughing. Besides, both knew the kid could swim.

As soon as the smaller boy dragged himself up the muddy shoulder of the wallow, he straightened to wring himself like a drenched dog. Then his eyes widened further. Frantic hands patted his clothing. Unsnapping the breast pocket of his uniform shirt, Bob One cursed.

Extracting his cell, he shook it, too. He flipped its screen. Nothing.

"Shit!" Taking offense, he yelled, "Stop laughing!"

They only turned away, laughed harder.
Reluctantly, Bob Two eventually followed Belmar toward their destination, though he must grip his aching sides to keep himself upright.

Ultimately, he told his younger coworker, "Mister Dunkin told you to leave it behind, dumbass, but you don't ever listen to nobody else!"

Segment 10

"I forgot!" Bob One followed only when he began to fear being left behind. So far as he could tell, only the boss could find their way home again. "That's a thousand bucks down the drain!"

"I'm not going to miss it, boy-o," announced a fully winded Belmar, once more waddling through the swamp, "which brings me to the second kind of smarts. That's the kind of man who learns for himself using his own two hands."

"Or not," chuckled Two.

"Right," goaded Belmar, "though you easily could do, if you'd only pull your head out of your ass and put that damned thing down for an hour."

Angry with himself for being both forgetful and clumsy, One struck a furious pose to toss the offending electronics as far as possible. Then he humbled himself to reconsider the idea, instead returning the phone to his pocket while nursing secret hopes of its magical recovery. Snapping this shut, he morosely pouted, "I guess I have no choice now."

"I guess you don't," retorted a highly amused Two, so he could not help but add a second shot, prodding, "dumbass."

"Your mother is!"

Sensing the slip of a taut rope, Belmar growled, "Boys! Enough!"

"Yes, sir, Mister Dunkin," conceded Number Two, though he closed the deal with a rude gesture directed toward his brooding cohort.

Presently, their guide paused atop a semidry hummock of swamp weeds and creepers. He studied the lie of the land for a time, comparing dull-green recesses of the hollow to the photographs of his memory.

When he could no longer tolerate an insect-buzzing silence, Bob One asked, "How's the second kind get paid, boss?"

Two guessed, "The second kind pays itself, dude."

A moment of silence followed, and then One asked, "Is that right, Mister Dunkin?"

"Most definitely," grunted Belmar.

Having oriented himself against the terrain, he realized they had arrived at the indicated destination. Over the course of several weeks, he had been mapping scat samples and molted skin sheds to track the animal he wanted next. This basin seemed to contain its primary haunts.

"This is it, fellahs," he announced, refusing to acknowledge the kids' grumbles.

While they had demonstrated their courage and skill with the animals, both being senior herpetology majors at FSU, both knew enough to show a healthy respect for their intended target. Bob One worked particularly hard to dissuade his mentor of his crazy plans. Only the money had lured them into the swamp that day.

Turning the gloom of cypress overhang, the Bobs surveyed large swaths of open water interspersed with hummocks like the one that supported them at present. Large old-growth cypress trees towered into the heavens to tangle the light and mar the day. Everything hung with moss, ivies and creepers. The air steamed and teemed with zipping, darting birds and insects, the former often hunting and feeding upon the latter.

While he allowed them to absorb the prospects of their immediate future, Belmar spoke with a distracted tone saying, "With a bit of effort, both types of smarts can get to the same place – more or less – since the apex of each pursuit is some kind of mastery. Most people think a PhD or MD earns well, and they do, but any man in Florida with a bit of ambition and skill can earn as much – maybe more, since nobody sues an air-conditioning serviceman for millions at a time."

"So," drawled Two, "as I recall you saying, this is a business that walks in both worlds. Book-smarts and other-smarts."

"Well, I think so, Bob Two," returned Belmar with an equally loquacious southern slant. "Summertime, you get the sunshine and wide-open spaces. The rest of the year, it's nothing but plush schoolwork and an excess of poontane."

Both Bobs blushed. He suspected the younger one might be a virgin – then again, he thought Bob One had a bit of a crush on Bob Two. Bob Two, naturally, remained oblivious.

Swallowing his fear and puffing his chest, One preoccupied himself by asking, "How does the second kind get paid, then?"

"Same as the other, like a commodity. The primary difference being the source of value accrued to a transaction. For the first kind, value is hidden inside the head. For the second, it's visible within the hands."

"Or it will be," produced Two grimly, "once we snatch this big mother."

"Right. This is the place, I think." Belmar stooped to shuck his pack and shotgun before he unthreaded the lacings of his boots. "Last one in performs the necropsy."

To their credit, neither Bob hesitated to follow. By now, they had soloed countless snatches and all three had worked as a team on several dozen very large captures. If successful, their latest hunt should mark a record for the season – maybe for all time, if Belmar's intuition proved to be correct.

Segment 10

Bob One set his gear aside to flex his toes in the rough sawgrass and sedge that everywhere grew raucously and with tenacious desperation. Clapping his hands together as though preparing for an icy plunge, he chanted, "Five-hundred dollars. Five-hundred dollars. Five-hundred dollars."

"Five-hundred, split between the two of you," reminded Belmar, "and only if she's as big as I think she is. We split the FWC commission evenly, three ways."

"That's another hundred a piece, if she's gravid," spouted Two as he eased off of the peat-logged limestone ridge and into the murky, waist-deep water.

"Yeah, I could almost buy one full credit hour of tuition with wages like that," scoffed Two.

"Just wait until you finish a master's and then a doctorate," encouraged Belmar sarcastically, having followed One into the water, so his toes raked the muck for slithery spoils.

"That's when we start earning the big bucks, right, Mister Dunkin."

"I don't know, since I'm not one, but I'm certain my advisor, a tenured professor, makes at least twenty-five dollars an hour." More droll sarcasm, of course. He motioned for the kids to spread out and then, once they complied, he motioned them further apart. This was going to be a whopper!

Bob One whistled appreciatively. "That's a lot. Right?"

Two made a motion as though gripping his friend's throat to slap the youth's face repeatedly back and forth. "That's about fifty-thou a year. Chump-change!"

Belmar wondered where Bob Two lived. Then he wondered how much the kid thought he would earn as a fish-and-game warden. So many hard lessons to learn in youth, he silently mused, sweeping his feet side-to-side with each slow step.

One answered, "It's about forty-grand more than I made last year. I bet it's enough to move out of my parents' house."

"If you want to live in a box and walk to work," retorted the bigger kid, his body moving in imitation of his mentor's. Secretly, he dreaded the encounter – as he did each time that they worked a snatch – but this part of the business attracted his interest more than any other. He reveled in the thrill and the terror of a life-and-death struggle with nature, one of the few that remained available to modern humankind.

When he returned to campus, he would tell war stories. Some chicks – the kind of chicks that he liked – would be impressed. He felt certain of this. At least, he hoped.

"Remember," coached Belmar, speaking slowly and distinctly, "we only get top dollar for a pristine hide. If we want to get paid, we need to work this one by the book. Cool and easy. No panic."

"I still think we need another guy," groused Bob One, "maybe two or three. If she's as big as you say."

"Oh, she's a porker. You can believe that. Twenty-five feet, alright, and maybe four-hundred pounds. At least."

"That's a hundred-thirty pounds each," complained One, though he continued walking the transect while pinching muck with timorous toes.

"Yeah, but five-hundred bucks divided by six is an ugly number, too. A guy can't even get laid with that kind of bankroll."

"You couldn't get laid with the whole sum," chided his younger friend.

"I bet I could get laid if I paid your mother," teased Two. "I hear she mastered the hand-job in middle school."

"Dude. Way too far."

"I know. I've seen your mother, remember?"

"I swear to god, Bob, I'm going to-."

"Hey! You two peanut-heads knock it off!" Belmar paused to draw his floppy hat away from his bristling pate, which he squeegeed with his free hand. "This is a full-on heads-out situation, now. If we slip up and this thing gets a hold of us, the *best* outcome is a lost payday. The worst case is a porker's feast. Got it?"

"Sure, Mister Dunkin," Bob Two answered for both young men, as usual.

Bob One grumbled. "We need a boat."

Segment 10

SEGMENT 11

Slatted eyes all eyelashes and clotted sleep, Sam smacked a rancid mouth to scratch a dew-slimed belly. What had become of his shirt? His boots? Why was he awakening on his porch?

Moving sedately, he lifted his right arm to rub his eyes open. A sound of tinkling glass resulted before he heard an empty bottle trundle across his porch floorboards with a hollow sound that ended with a drop into weeds grown ramshackle all around.

"Oh, yeah," he grumped. Smacking his tongue against the roof of his mouth again, he yawned, ground his eyeballs with both fists, and then pushed his back up against an awning support column. Through blurry eyes, he marked the first hint of sunrise. Birds and insects began to awaken, raucous and hungry. "I don't remember drinking the whole bottle."

Next, he considered his purpose of the previous evening. He had been drinking for courage. Courage to do *the deed*.

"Did we do it, Jen?" he wondered aloud.

No way of telling, he thought. The night might have gone either way. Reconsidering with a stiffened stretch and another yawn, he knew better.

"You never had any balls," he griped, his voice and tone that of his father's, these many years dead. "Never any guts. And no brains, neither! Shit!"

His eyes opened wider so he could properly hate himself. To do that, he needed to absorb the many harsh realities of his chosen lifestyle. In particular, he needed to hate the house and its claustrophobic, swamp-bound holler. For hating the house, he could hate his father, and his father's father. All the way back to the misty dawn of time, maybe, his familial line poisoned by its choice of women, generation upon generation.

An uncertain gaze settled on his naked toes. Where had he left his socks?

Mud caked his legs to mid-calf. His hands, too.

When he managed to present a coordinated focus, Sam's attention shifted forward to the bowed and splintered wood of his porch deck. A hundred years old, some of those planks might be. Bent when his daddy had worn diapers.

Paint cracked and peeled off everything. Nothing seemed whole or polished or new. Everything, rundown. Secondhand. Like him. Like his entire familial line, which would die with him.

"I'm the last of the great American screw-ups," he told his toes, which wiggled to crinkle the filthy crust that had dried there. "A prodigal son of shit."

She arrived in '77. Lon brought her home near the end of summer. They married in the fall.

Two years later, Sam sat in the docket. Lon lay in a casket. Cassandra Lee Seminole nee Winchell rested comfortably at home. Her home, by then. Free and clear and legal and no criminal charges pending. No day in court due her.

Segment 11

Demon Worm

Sitting straighter, Sam shuttered bloodshot eyes to groan and grunt rheumatically, his bones aching for their hard night's rest. To himself and the memories replaying across the backs of his eyelids, he announced, "Oh, they knew the truth. Those state investigators, they knew. The county boys, too. For sure, the chief knew."

He sniffled. "But knowing ain't proving."

Staring past his toes into the steaming swamp that brooded just across the length of his tumble-down front porch, Sam felt vaguely disturbed by the lie of things. Never a fun place to be, something seemed decidedly wrong about his current perspective.

It's the booze. The hangover. The hard bed. The sticky dew. That endless reek of death and decay from the swamp. Sounds of real-life horror. Everywhere.

"Nothing simple," he moaned hatefully, "nothing easy. Especially that which should be simple and easy."

Life shouldn't be so hard, he groused. A man should be able to stay on track without so much effort.

"Everything starts in awe," he commiserated to Jen, "same as the break of day. Brilliant sunbeams make diamonds of dust motes, so a body feels the power and the glory. Everything alive. Everything breathing."

Now he shook his head. He wished for more whiskey. Then he immediately hated himself for his desire, so his stomach rolled emptily, silently screaming, '*No more!*'.

"Round about lunchtime, the heat of midday settles down on a man's shoulders," he continued despondently, his gaze a blurred smear of watery green, "so life gets to be work. Hell, I knew that, Jen, as soon as I was old enough to curse properly."

He knew work in the bayou, of course – whatever daddy and pappy needed done of a particular day. Too, he

Segment 11

understood the work of schoolbooks and written lessons, though he never excelled there. Yet, for Sam-the-Youth, back then in the golden 'Seventies, work meant football.

Southern Florida football. Nobody plays ball the way southern boys play the game. Rough. Tumble. Merciless on the field and vaunted in the high school hallways, as a running back and linebacker, Sam Dell had done well for himself.

"I was the only one in my class to get a full ride to FSU," he told Jen, her black eyes staring back at him from the blur stretching wide just beyond the length of his toes. "Of course, the team helped, since we had a winning season during my junior and senior terms, but it was me that won the MVP both years. I set and broke a dozen records along the way. You know I did, Jen," he gushed, sucking a snootful of dewy snot to punctuate.

Jen's flat, black eyes stared back. Lifeless and dull in her state of irrevocable mortality. Gone forever.

He left his cramped home for the first time in '76, vowing never to return. Of course, winter holidays are always hungry holidays for homeless youth.

Momma was still alive back then. She fed him. Tried to keep him safe from pops whenever the Southern Comfort spilled too deep. Pappy, too, when he could, but the old man was years dead by then.

"I had to come back in the summer of 'Seventy-Seven," he gloomed unhappily. Jen glared back at him, silent and unresponsive. Judging, perhaps condemning him. Her unblinking eyes sparkled meanly. "I had no choice, but it was only for a few months. Only for that first year. I was certain to get a do-nothing campus job through the next summer. Coach promised. My numbers were that good."

He had won no awards that first season on the gridiron, but he had started more than once. He had held his own, too, and daddy nowhere to be seen. Just sex, drugs and rock-n-roll music.

"I always missed Lon," he confessed to his lifeless companion. "He was the best part about coming back." Sam chuckled so his belly rolled and his head lolled against the hard wood of the support column. "The man never blamed me for leaving, you know. I tried and tried, of course, but I could never convince him to come away with me. For some strange reason that I could never understand, Lonnie loved this place. Everything about it pleased him. The stink, too."

Jen slithered closer, her movements wraith-like and silent atop the floorboards. In cold death, she presented a patched shadow of her former self. That hypnotic gaze dominated, pupils inky black and forever deep.

By '79, everything seemed to be going well. Too good to be true, pondered Sam.

"A tryout with the Dolphins seemed a sure-thing," he boasted, reaching for a bottle that had gone missing. He snapped muddy fingers, denied. "I only needed to play healthy one more year to make the A-Team."

Then Lon called him home again. "A party," gushed Sam, those deep black eyes staring back at him from almost forty years deep in time, "an anniversary celebration with a special announcement."

He pulled his legs closer to double his knees inside grasping arms. Jen only watched from her shrouds of death, moving slow and easy the way the dead will do.

"They sent the invitation in April," he continued sloppily, sniffling to rub and clear blurred eyes, "just so I could for certain be there in June. Just one week of my life.

Segment 11

That's all. A single step along a bright and promising path, and all the love of Jesus shining through."

Sam sat straighter that he might more directly wallow in the misery of his condition. Morning lifted shadows from the 'glades, so cypress crowns prompted thoughts of heavenly delights. Jenny scarcely marveled.

"I could've said 'no'," he lamented. "I had all the women I needed. More. Beautiful women, every single one of them. All way above Dell-family paygrade, even if none of them were *her*. Any one of them, a first-class ticket out of this shitty place!"

He would have been gone forever. Months away.

"Only, small places have a way of keeping a person. Of calling him back when he has the gall to leave. Of roping him in when he has a mind to stray. Like a jealous lover or an obsessive enemy. The draw of it is relentless and its attention is never absent."

Even when long gone, a person's reputation lingers with his or her family. Anyway, the prodigal offspring must return home from time to time. Or not. Either response marks a man. Good or bad.

For most, it's a funeral. One of the lucky, the hapless heir had escaped only to be drawn back for the settlement of family affairs. Debts to repay. Some with blood. Then one transgression follows another until too much has passed. Too much love or lust. Too much hate. Too much time.

"Too much *her*," he guttered viciously, spitting bile with each syllable.

Oh, that summer had not marked the first incident of their acquaintanceship. He had known her since his best friend brought her home.

Except, June '79 marked the first time that Cass had paid close attention to Sam Dell, in turn. "It was no small wonder," he confessed simply, "because me and Lon were opposites in almost every way."

Lon had been a great man. Of personality and character. Of every good thing, it seemed to Sam. Where the latter stood short and stocky, Lonnie stood tall and lean of muscle, a golden god of the bayous. Sam grew pasty and hairy, while Lon enjoyed his aboriginal heritage, which included just enough color to highlight green eyes and bronzed skin. Everything about the man shaped an attractive contrast, while Sam had always just been Sam. Good ol' Sam.

Not so smart. Not so lucky. Not so good looking.

Everyone loved or hated Lon Seminole. Nobody much noticed Sam Dell at all, not even for his standout performances on the gridiron. Not when he stood alongside his best friend, anyway.

"But I was okay with that, Jen, even after I came back from school," he mused sullenly, speaking directly into Jenny's grave-bound gaze. "I never lorded it over him, or resented him, nor none of that. 'Cause we was friends, girl. *Best* friends. Brothers, even. And he wasn't like that, either. He was good. Honest. Loyal. He never done me wrong or spoke an ill word – unless I deserved it, mind you."

He had deserved such treatment, too. From time to time. Sam Dell never possessed or understood his friend's unbending sense of morality. Rules were something to break.

"Nobody snuck evil past Lon Seminole though." Once more, Sam's hand flexed for an absent bottle and he wish-denied himself a thirst for further drink so early in the morning. Jen's black eyes mocked him without movement, but she could not – *would* not – provide him further succor. Everything appeared cold and hard in death. "That's what killed him more than anything else, Jen. His sense of right and wrong. 'Cause everyone sees the world through the lens of themselves, don't they? Everyone sees a reflection of what they know. Everything else is just scenery. If it doesn't seem to exist, then it just isn't, that's all."

He would never believe evil of his young bride. Why should he?

She was all smiles and sweet kisses in his presence. When his back turned, a demon zipped itself out of her skin to prowl about moonlit Everglade eves in search of an itch to scratch.

That summer, him living so close, she came slinking around the very porch that held Sam's reclined corpulence through yet another inglorious sunrise. "And me sipping Crown Cola in a swing that used to stand right yonder," he pointed to the far end of the porch, just where Jen's tail gently waggled, "wearing blue-jeans and tanned flesh and not an ounce of fat on me."

Sure, he had known her from before. He could not help but obsess on her every shimmering movement whenever the woman lingered in his presence. Lon knew, of course. He couldn't care less, since he never feared his best friend. They never ate from the same bowl, the two of them, no matter how successful Sam Dell might be.

"Lon always shined brighter," he mumbled sloppily, "but I never minded so much, since he shared fully everything with me, holding nothing back for himself. He would pass most girls to me whenever the notion struck the two of us, yet he could never understand the idea of needing a thing completely, himself. He never had such needs."

Nothing to share. Not one hour to spare.

"I never knew I had to have her, Jen," he blubbered, her black eyes glinting with his unhappy reflection, "until she wanted me, in turn. Leastwise, this was her promise. A promise of every good thing, all shining golden in the sun and full of ten-thousand blessed days, endless hours, spent with her. Ever for *her*." He spat the last syllable.

Jen's head froze. She licked rancid lips. Watching.

Across the horizon-bending expanse of her black eyes, he relived his dreams and his nightmares, too. Dreams of her returning again and again to his bedroom, her secret visitations of a moonlit night intended to dispel his fears and embolden his courage. Nightmares of the same treatment, since each day afterward he must confront his friend as a walking, breathing lie. As a slithering, crawling betrayal.

That summer, everything spoiled. Sam Dell started to rot, though he would live many decades longer, each day a torment. In absence of his slain best friend. In absence of her. More wickedly, in *presence* of her, too.

So close. "So far," he moaned.

Jen agreed. She lifted her gaze to match the level of Sam's dull, glazed eyes. Together, eyeballs-to-eyeballs, the two of them communed in silent, frozen wonder.

"She worked me through each week of that summer, long past the party, long after I should have returned to campus for pre-season training camp." Sam pulled his knees closer. Jen grinned like a hyena to mock this gesture of self-pity, her pink mouth gaping wide and her snigger formed into a snide hiss. "What's the price of a man's life? Better, what's the price of a promising young man's future? Its entire value, cashed like a bad check with a single phone call."

He never went back to school. They held a slot for him the following fall, but he didn't go back then, either.

Segment 11

"By that time, it was too late," he brooded. He couldn't go back. Ever. Afterward, he couldn't move forward either.

"It's a scarlet letter, that's what. Ain't it, Jen? The mark of Cain to follow a man wherever he goes thereafter. No washing it off. No scrubbing it clean. Years of wear make no difference and they never let you forget."

Of course, five years in a Southern Florida penitentiary is something the man, himself, can never forget either. He ruminated and pondered.

"Maybe that's why it never washes away," he wondered, once more reaching for a missing bottle.

This time, Jen reacted without caution. She reared back, hissing angrily, and then she rose two full feet, so her head hung over the reclined Sam Dell like a menacing stalk.

That set the man's eyes to watering. Curious. Curious and strange, he thought, how Jen's eyes never blinked. In all this time, despite the glare of sunshine, never a flinch or a flicker.

In a maddened moment, his alcohol-steeped vision cleared and he recognized the camouflaged thing that loomed over him. *Hot shit!*

Drawling, "*Gaw-aaawww-awd* damn!" Sam rolled hard right. In the same moment, a giant demon worm lunched forward to bite him across his face and initiate the coil-and-swallow routine that so often filled its vast, ravenous gut.

Instead, its mass struck the porch rail with a solid impact that shuddered the entire house. Sam tumbled against the front wall, his feet scrambling for purchase to lift his body up and away from his porch deck. There, he watched a fantastically large snake recover from its death-lunge to make a coiling ball of its form, clearly intending to make another play for breakfast.

Recalling the spry days of his athletic youth, Sam somehow found himself running across the front wall of his rundown shack, so he flung himself over the railing and into the sawgrass, a terror-powered superhero. Charging around back, he ran so fast to the rear door of his house that the movement passed like some kind of hillbilly teleportation.

No matter how quickly the former halfback MVP ran, he could not fetch his pistol quickly enough. By the time he returned to his front porch, she had disappeared into the swamp.

Sam panted, staggered by fright and expended effort. Though he stalked the full circumference of his wrap-around porch, he found no sign of that scaly demon. Accordingly, he began to question his memory. Perhaps the serpent and the devil had incarnated itself in the same beast there on his porch, a sign of things to come, a reminder of the she-devil that he had failed to slay during the previous evening.

"Blood demands blood," he whispered, his tone ragged and worn. Almost, he convinced himself of the nightmare within a nightmare.

Then he noticed a wet trail curled along warped floorboards, ending where sedge slowly recovered from a deep crush. In that moment, he thought of Jen-Jen and that hideous lump hidden within the snake's belly.

Licking lips, his hands trembling, Sam breathed harshly, softly repeating, "*God damn.*"

Segment 11

SEGMENT 12

This would be his last trip. Already a week overdue on campus, Bob One had collected a host of reasons to say so. Worse yet, a storm approached, so they were sure to get wet if the hunt ran long – and they always ran long. If necessary, come Sunday evening and an empty sack, he would get loud and angry.

After all, this would mark their fourth weekend sacrifice, and they had collected nothing to show for their efforts. Their rate of return rapidly diminished, while their prospects for success improved not at all.

Besides, Bob One resented being 'Bob One'. As per ritual, he followed his so-called mentor across the apron of 'Bailey's Corner Store', having started the pump to fuel Belmar's truck for the day. While yet another wasted Saturday morning crowned through cypress forest. *I should still be asleep, god damn it!*

Angrily, he mumbled, "My name is Roberto, asshole." Roberto Andres Morales. The third. "*Pinche pendejo.*" Pronounced *pin-shay pen-de-ho*, with lots of phlegm emphasizing the '*de-ho*' part.

Nobody called him 'Bob', at all, except that stupid peckerwood, Belmar Dunkin. If he hadn't heard the wrong name in the first place, the dumbass would have no need to add the label 'One'. So, we would have Roberto and

Robert, or Roberto and Bob, if the other guy was okay with being 'number two'. Whatever.

Following Bob Two through the front door of the store, a door chime marked the forfeit of his day. He translated, growling, "Stupid asshole."

This label basically meant the same thing as *pinche pendejo*, except Roberto recognized an additional fluidity to the latter term. Much like the f-word could be used as an English noun, verb, adverb, gerund and every other part of speech, his use of these 'native' terms could present different meanings when used in varied contexts. Today, everything translated to 'stupid asshole'.

Bailey greeted the three with too much joy given the early hour and overcast skies. When he remarked upon the wisdom of wading for snakes in the swamp with a vast storm approaching, Belmar made excuses and Bob Two boasted moronically. Roberto only fumed silently at slack southern stupidity.

Once inside, Bob Two moved directly toward the soda machine. *What a fat jerk.*

He seemed to tolerate the abuse. The mocking pet names. The lack of pay. The muck and fecal matter. Everything 'boss' said went down like gospel. Belmar-the-Golden-Swamp-God spoke and Bob Two cleaved-unto, horny and pliable.

All summer long, Roberto heard nothing but Belmar-this and Belmar-that and, "Belmar can smoke his own bone." This bit, he added himself, grumbling under his breath.

The god, himself, stopped at the store's minimalistic coffee bar. Lots of sugar and cream. *White man's cocaine.*

Of course, Roberto identified as an American and nothing more, but his dark hair and darker eyes clearly

Demon Worm

marked him for his Cuban ancestry. Bob Two and Belmar shared origins in the 'Glades, both of them like cypress sprouts dropped at the roots of their sires. Number Two stood as tall as his beloved mentor and Christ-like savior, but the younger man's form added at least a hundred pounds of muscle and fat. Save for thicker hair and chubbier, softer features all around, the two of them might be cousins.

"They probably are," he breathed softly, speaking only to himself, "since their grandmas and grandpas have been humping each other through countless genetically-twisted generations." *They seem to get pastier and uglier every year.*

No matter what happened this weekend though, Bob One vowed this trip would be his last. The same time next weekend would find him tucked into his sheets, sawing logs and cutting farts.

While retracting a sugar-free hydrating beverage from a cooler situated in the store's farthest corner, he wondered how long some of these offerings had been waiting for a sale. The locals rarely bothered with anything other than southern staples, these chiefly being soda, coffee, iced tea and, of course, beer. Sometimes whiskey, but never before noon on a Sunday, for some weird reason.

Unlike Bob Two and his homo-erotic hero, Roberto came from one of the more affluent Miami suburbs. These weekend trips into the bush – indeed, the entire summer internship – had developed into a much more frightening and unpleasant experience than he had naively anticipated prior to accepting the gig. To be fair, Belmar had not misrepresented the hardships that he had endured, nor had he too generously described the pay.

Yet neither had he said anything about... *all that!* He watched his best friend play grab-ass and make lewd jokes with their older companion and supervisor. Their behavior disturbed a rack of snack foods, which they must restore to proper order, giggling and snorting as though engaged in a comical cabal.

To the uninitiated, this would appear to be good, clean fun. Man-on-man horseplay.

Roberto saw something else, something disturbing and discomfiting. Especially in light of Belmar's continued and obvious relationship with Crazy Cat Lady. Clearly, the man played both sides of the field with equal deftness.

Bob One could not possibly hope to compete. Since Bob Two seemed to be completely unaware of his own thrall.

"I hate him," Roberto groused quietly. *Which?*

Fishing his back pocket for a wallet, he approached the counter. There, the proprietor awaited their pleasure, having perched his rotund mass atop a frustrated stool that groaned and creaked beneath him.

"Hey, there, Belmar," called Bailey, the store-guy, "you two cut the shit before I bill you for half my inventory as damaged goods!"

"Sorry Mister Bailey," called Belmar, "I haven't had my coffee, yet."

Roberto stood before the register, his drink on the counter and a five-spot dangling from his fingertips. Bailey only sat atop the stool, arms folded and eyes twinkling. A big, stupid grin spread across his face.

When the man repeatedly jutted his chin as though to prompt an unknown remark, Bob One grumpily demanded, "What?"

Rather than address the college boy, Bailey again called to Belmar, asking, "Is this them? Your snake catcher twins?"

Bob One scowled. "Mister, if you think we're twins, then you need to have your head checked. I don't even know that giant asshole."

"Oooh," teased Bob Two, "somebody woke up too early!"

He dropped his soda onto the counter next to his best friend's choice. The bottle's cap, already opened, fizzed excitedly to ooze trickles of cola that traced runways through growing beads of perspiration.

"Bob One and Bob Two, is it?" wondered the old man perched atop the tripod. "Let me guess... you're the runner and you're he-who-gets-squeezed. I bet I nailed it, didn't I?"

Having appropriately identified the two younger men, Bob One glowered while Bob Two grinned idiotically. Belmar added a steaming cup of coffee to their collective purchase, chuckling to confirm, "Oh, yeah. This is the man who outran a demon worm."

Roberto's face glowed bright red. His expression collapsed the way a sunny day clouds for a sudden storm.

Turning to confront his 'boss', his tone accusatory and too pathetic, he whined, "You told him I shit my pants!"

Belmar jerked backward as though struck by an odd thought. Then he laughed, "No, but you did, sucker."

His two supposed 'friends' laughed together. Bailey-the-Store-Guy laughed, too.

Then the latter's diplomatic nature asserted itself in the face of a paying customer's distress, so he softened the fun by adding, "Ah, hells-bells, boy. Don't take it so hard. Just about anybody would mess themselves in the same situation. I know I would."

"Yeah, Toe," this being Bob One's pet name for his friend, "don't worry about it. I peed myself a bit, too, I think."

"I know you did," gushed Belmar, bending double to recall the worst and most terrifying moment of Bob One's entire life, "because, afterward, I felt a warm spot in the water!"

Fuming, Roberto spun on a heel to stalk angrily through the door. He attempted to slam it behind him, a gesture frustrated by stubborn hydraulics. This display only made his hateful audience laugh harder, louder and longer.

He really had crapped himself that day, though he remained completely unaware of having done so until hours later, given the general stink of swamp muck. Long after they had euthanized and recovered their prize python, indeed, perhaps an hour after they had started their drive home, the smell caught up with them in the confined cab of Belmar's truck.

Naturally, he had heard about this having happened to others and he had seen the same performance on a variety of nature-shows, but he had never understood the reflexive nature of the act. It had happened without conscious thought or recognition.

He suspected it must be nature's way of lightening the load for a fight-or-flight response, or perhaps the smell served to deter would-be predators. Either way, Roberto thought his detractors had missed the point.

According to his enraged understanding, he stopped in the parking lot to spin on his heel, ball his fists, stamp his foot and screech, "Nobody expects to be food! Jerks!"

Lions and tigers and bears, he thought. Everyone knows these beasts can be man eaters. "Snakes really do kill and consume people," he groused, turning to confront

Segment 12

the claustrophobic holler that sheltered the crossroads and Bailey's Corner Store the way a green cathedral overawes an asphalt altar, "grown adults, even."

That particular snake had been very large. Very hungry. Very aggressive.

Even though it had obviously eaten recently, that green porker had charged him with a ravenous anger. It almost caught him!

Once more reliving a lifetime in a minute, Roberto imagined the feel of the serpent's crush, its fangs working their way along his body like a ratchet, progressing from head to feet. Inch upon inch. Coiling and squeezing. Gulping and swallowing.

Then, inside the beast. Suffocating. Helpless.

Segment 12

SEGMENT 13

Bob Two stood on the front apron of Bailey's Corner Store, his warming soda dripping sweat from the grip of one beefy fist. He watched his friend watching him from inside the stifling cab of Belmar's truck. Pouting. Staring back at him, hurt and wounded and pouting.

Overhead, fully visible only amid a large hollow that engulfed the crossroads market, he recognized the drear roll of a Southern Florida gully-washer. Sometime in the next day or two the 'Glades would flood. Or not.

As with Roberto's fickle mood, only guesswork gauged the doom. Today seemed a black day, but time would tell.

Belmar joined him beyond the threshold, calling his goodbyes while teasing the old man by repeatedly referring to him as 'Mister Bailey'. Everyone knew the guy's family name since they collectively owned half the county.

"I swear," hissed Bob Two, masking the movement of his lips by pausing to sip from his uncapped soda bottle, "sometimes he acts just like a woman scorned."

Grinning mischievously, happy to have goaded the snotty little bastard yet again, Belmar purred, "Do you ever wonder why?"

"I know why," asserted Bob Two. "He's a little bitch. Always has been. Since grade school, even."

So late in the summer, Belmar had yet to properly place the Bobs. He thought he understood them one moment, only to revise his opinion the next. Largely, he wondered about Two. The man seemed oblivious most days, while on others he appeared to know exactly what he was doing, tweaking and twisting the smaller man's delights and insights.

Something about their dynamic seemed perverse. Closeted. Mutually abusive, yet mutually dependent.

Never a mention of other companions. Weird.

Despite sunrise, the temperature rose suddenly. Dropping through treetop gaps, a wild gust swirled dust and debris around their ankles. Then all as quickly fell still again, and the stifling humidity returned.

Pondering rain, Belmar led his Number Two across the lot to a row of pumps, where he worked to disengage the nozzle while Bob replaced the truck's gas cap. He watched Bob Two's efforts, pondering the size of his hands and boots. Wondering.

Aloud, he mused, "Maybe we should stop by Cat Lady's place tonight. We might snag a shower and a beer on the way back to town."

Finishing his minor task, Bob Two straightened to confront his supervisor. Sure, he recognized that light in the other's eyes, but its implications only served to vaguely frighten him. The same kind of attention from a female scared him, too. In the same way. For the same reasons.

Regardless of his fears, he felt emboldened by the wildness of the 'Glades and by the base, earthy philosophies espoused among those who lived there. Unreadable as always, he stood before Belmar, neither shrinking nor inviting, his demeanor outwardly oblivious.

Enigmatically, Two nodded. "She seems fun."

Belmar cocked a curious head. "Right."

Shifting his floppy campaign hat atop the dome of his bristling head, Belmar maneuvered around his intern to take his place behind the truck's wheel. *Maybe a bit of whiskey and some grass would loosen their collars*, he thought. Then he wondered if his young companions had tried either vice.

Bob Two recognized all these suspicions, but he could formulate no reply. In his home, the home of Big John the Baptist, such topics never arose, all marking questions he never asked and answers he never had.

Oh, he understood the mechanism and the biology well enough, but he thought gross human affection should represent the outcome of a lifelong match. In turn, a lifelong match should strike a man thunderously with all the might and fury of the lord. For all his looking, then, Bob Two had never encountered the shining brilliance that he expected to reveal Jesus in such a moment.

Watching Belmar return to his pickup, his lanky, angular body scarcely filling his khaki uniform, Bob Two thought he might not be an unhandsome man. Being a male, himself, he felt unqualified to make an accurate assessment, but he knew Crazy Cat Lady had taken a quick shine to boss.

Surrendering this effort with a shrug, Two walked around the bed of the truck to join his best friend in its cab. Clearly, Roberto intended to pout. Knowing his friend well, Bob Two expected this treatment to last for perhaps five minutes since Roberto could never shut-up and since he had no stomach for unpleasantness of any kind. Most times.

Taking his place beside Toe, he offered his companion the abandoned drink. Stiffly, the smaller man accepted. Angrily, he twisted its top. Vehemently, he drank. Pouting.

Belmar watched this display while hovering over the truck's ignition, keys ready but untwisted. Smiling ruefully, he shook his head.

Confronting a long day, he sighed leadenly, waxing apologetic. Gently, he insisted, "I really didn't say a thing about that part of it, Roberto. Honest."

Bob One's lower lip quivered. "I know."

"There's no shame in it, you know, since-."

"I don't want to talk about it." One drink sealed his statement, case closed.

Belmar shrugged. "Sure, Bob. Only, this is a head-out situation, remember? Total focus? If you're distracted or feeling less than part of the team, then-."

"I'm fine!" When this statement sounded too forced, Bob One sucked a deep, lung-filling breath, which he then blew long and slow through puckered lips. "I just... I just don't want to talk about it. Really. I'm fine."

An awkward moment settled over the three of them. Since he truly felt concerned for their group dynamic, Belmar released the keys to leave them dangling from the truck's ignition. He leaned backward, twisting his body to confront his two interns more directly, so his arm crossed behind Bob One's head to line the seatback, all three sitting astride the cab's lone bench.

"Listen up, camper," he spoke with a gentle yet forceful tone, "I think you've missed a few clues along the way this summer. Maybe your hopes steer you another way or blind you to the truth, but you need to know something, and you need to know it with startling clarity. I'm heterosexual. I suspect your pal is, too."

Upon hearing these last two statements, Roberto's eyes popped. His face paled. Verged on another sip, his mouth hung open, so he seemed ready to vomit.

"No matter what you think you see, I'm not hitting on Bob Two, here, and I'm not trying to take him away from you. When this summer internship ends for you, I'm going back to grad school and you're going back to your senior year. Truly, we're not playing the same game at all."

Bob Two groaned. When Roberto began scrambling in a frenetic and undirected manner, his arms and legs flailing, Bob knew exactly what his friend needed.

Obliging, he opened his door to exit the cab. Roberto immediately bolted, leaping from the truck to stalk across the parking lot and onto the two-lane roadway, clearly bound to walk all the way home. This time, for real.

Leaning through his open window, Belmar called, "Hey, Bob, come on back, man! It's not a problem, really! I'm only trying to help!"

Though his shoulders bunched and his ears burned bright red, Bob One showed no sign of slowing or stopping. Without turning, he savagely screeched, "My name is Roberto, you redneck peckerwood asshole!"

Belmar blinked, taken aback. Softly, speaking to Bob Two, who yet lingered in the open passenger-side door, he announced, "Honestly, I didn't know the little guy had it in him. You curse more than he does, and you're the son of a preacher."

When Two said nothing, Belmar dipped his head low to make eye contact, given the obstruction of the truck's cab. He asked, "Should we go get him?"

Bob shook his head, resisting all insistence until boss surrendered. "It's no use. I know him. He's butt-sprung now, and no way of bending his attitude back into frame any time soon." The youth sighed leadenly and then returned to his place with a somber grunt. "You shouldn't have said that."

Belmar replied, "He has a crush on you."

Another sigh. Bob stared stiffly through the front windshield. "I know that. I guess I always have known."

"You never said anything about it? Ever?" The older man whistled, starting his truck and shifting to 'D' for 'Drive'. "And you've known each other, what? Fifteen years?"

"Something like that."

They drove away in silence. Then the silence lingered across several miles that filled their minds with dark thoughts the way endless cypress crowns filled the sky with tangled shadows. "I won't ask why, if it's worrying you."

Relaxing, at last, Bob practiced a cathartic mantra in silent prayer. He sipped his soda.

"I guess... I never felt the need to make that choice, myself," he confessed, his tone neutral but unrepentant.

"Your pops?"

Bob understood the question. "If I was, the old man wouldn't like it. I know that much, but I don't think he would hate me. Mom, neither. I guess if I wanted... that... I would eventually get right with it. Somehow. As would my family. Most of them."

Several more minutes transpired awkwardly. The swamp closed around the roadway until it swallowed them, a serpent gulping its meal. Whole.

"I shouldn't have interfered," offered the older man, his words somber, although his tone reflected a small matter of concern.

"No," enthused Bob, "you shouldn't have done."

"Then again," offered Belmar, "maybe you shouldn't have strung him out so long, either."

Segment 13

For a moment, the younger man bristled. Then his shoulders slumped. Hunching low, he peered into the side mirror, as though he might see his friend stomping northbound for home.

Again, he sighed heavily. "No, I guess not."

Several minutes further passed without speaking, until Belmar prompted, "What's next?"

Bob shrugged. "He'll get a ride home. We'll talk next week."

"He didn't want to be here today, anyway," guessed Belmar. "I could see it in his eyes. He looked tired."

"And frightened."

Belmar nodded. Having guessed as much, he had intended his reluctant silence to spare the boy's pride. Next, he anticipated Bob Two's follow-up question. "It's not so much fun with two, but it can be done. Chiefly, I make up for the missing pair of hands by drawing the pistol faster, if push comes to shove." When Bob appeared to doubt, he added, "Don't worry. We'll be fine."

The scenery streaming along as a green blur, they drove past Sam Dell's rundown homestead. His driveway also marked the overgrown cutoff that wended its way toward Cassie's place. Both heads turned to mark its passage, as though they might see into the distance and into the future with the same sight.

Bob licked bitter lips. He asked, "What about that thing with Cat Lady? Can you really make it work?"

Belmar grinned lecherously. He tipped his head.

"Probably."

Segment 13

SEGMENT 14

Nothing reminds a person of their worth better than tough times, thought Roberto. Resentment plumed like flames through flared nostrils as he stomped away from Belmar's truck. His gaze like a laser cut the pavement ahead of him. Curled nails pressed into the flesh of his palms, and he thought his thumb might break his fingers for its relentless constriction of his fists.

This is when he heard the truck motor start. As he listened to its bald tires rush away southward, he supposed Robert knew better than pursue him, begging. Though he rarely dropped off the deeper edge of human behavior, Roberto dove deep during those infrequent circumstances to resurface only days later.

"That's it!" he hissed evilly, stomping along. "I am over and done with Robert Johnathan Price, that big, fat *jerk!*"

Of course, the instant he pondered this schism, he must also confront the need to find a ride home. His friends were Robert's friends, and the division was never even. In fact, when he felt like being honest, he suspected they would all identify as Robert's companions if asked, only tolerating the inflexible Roberto for the other's sake.

Most people he met seemed little inclined to like him. Again, forcing himself to be honest, he admitted that *nobody* liked him.

Almost everyone liked Robert. The same way most people enjoy a precocious child. His naivety and unquestioning warmth welcomed all comers. Moths batting about a naked flame, everyone seemed to circle the man at least once upon first meeting him, if only to momentarily admire a rare thing in a common world.

Nobody circled the Flame of Roberto. Most consciously avoided his dark light. He could never accurately understand why, though he could guess.

Often, he attributed their dismissal, disregard and disrespect to jealously. Other character flaws figured large, as well. He rarely traced the source of such failures to a personal shortcoming of his own, of course, but not for lack of attempt. Truth be told, Roberto spent most waking hours analyzing himself for any slightest indication of such faults, so he knew himself in intricate detail and nowhere could he find such a fractious foundation.

True, he erred and he did so often, especially within social contexts. He might say or do the wrong thing at the right time, but these events he could easily trace to misunderstanding or ignorance. Usually, on the part of the offended party.

For example, today's unfortunate outcome obviously sourced in Belmar's closeted projections. Clearly gay while having been born into the type-A machismo of Southern Florida culture, the middle-aged wildlife agent simply could not accept his own deviant sexual orientation. When he played 'grab-ass' with Rob – AKA 'Bob Two' – the man clearly interpreted his actions as rough-and-tumble heterosexual interaction, while everyone else in the room no doubt emphasized the 'ass-grabbing' nature of their interplay.

How could he be so certain of the other's failures and weaknesses? Simple. Belmar had first mentioned homosexuality – not Roberto. Then the man had gone out of his way to stress his heterosexual interests, while also affirming those of his friend, Bob Two, although the latter had not asked for such support.

"Methinks thou doth protest too much," he seethed aloud, stomping along the cracked and potted edge of the two-lane asphalt roadway, bound north for some odd reason.

Hadn't the Nazis done the same thing? Hadn't those goons identified and isolated homosexuals among the population, forcing these dubious offenders to wear pink triangles as badges? All while chasing young men and boys in sporty jackboots or playing dress-up with a bunch of sycophantic, red-on-black-loving primps!

"*You're* the faggots!" he raggedly cried, stomping his feet and adding a demented screech of rage to punctuate.

No matter the vehemence of his denunciation, every syllable soaked into the descending cypress canopy. Nothing echoed or reverberated. His words simply disappeared with his breath. Impotent and wasted.

"Like everything else," he slumped.

When he tried to think who he might call for assistance with the long ride back to campus – someone who was not momma – Roberto drew a blank. A handful of cousins might do the job, *maybe*, but they lived so far away. He could not possibly impose upon them this way.

Besides, he self-confessed again, they wouldn't come. Probably, they would simply hang-up on him the moment they recognized the caller. Roberto's lower lip quivered.

He wondered why his best friend believed him to be gay. Why had Robert chosen Belmar over his old playmate from first-grade?

Segment 14

How pathetic! The latter only needed to make an indecent insinuation to break the former loose and trash a lifelong relationship.

Obviously, Robert – like Belmar – must be closeted, too. This thought passed through Roberto's mind with an indelicate tingle. The possibilities intrigued, and he again pondered countless memories of his friend's large, manly hands and feet. His golden smile. Green eyes.

Roberto swallowed stiffly. Once more, his conscience traced the wires of a psychological spider's web, one that charted his bizarre thoughts to valid, non-disturbing interpretations. All men considered such ideations from time to time, he silently counseled himself. Throughout the course of such debates, only actions mattered.

Who had been grabbing which ass? *That's right!*

Still, he already missed his friend's comforting companionship. Growing up in the same system, though born of opposite economic prospects, Robert's hulking presence and nonjudgmental style had avoided or remedied so many frightening problems for the smaller man. He had come to depend upon Robert more like a security blanket. A friend, too, of course. Not like a lover.

Also true, Roberto sometimes pondered scintillating fantasies that involved dorm-room wrestling matches and loose shorts. He empathized the soft, warm, yielding, stiffness of certain body parts not his own, how these might feel pulsating within his grip or bouncing atop his palms. Too, he rarely dreamed of violent assault, of being used abusively and repeatedly by another for hours upon hours through the night until sunrise screamed mercy and the world drowned in rancid sweat.

All, natural ideations as he understood human nature to be. All perfectly harmless.

Segment 14

Since he had never acted upon such deviant fantasies. Since he had never incorporated such outreach into the coursework of his day-to-day life. Since he had resisted the urge to masturbate for days – sometimes weeks – at a time. More particularly, since he almost never thought of Robert Price during rare, self-administered climaxes.

Instead, these tended to be faceless moments dominated by formless thrusting, moderate pain, and anonymous penetrations. As such, Roberto understood these aberrant incidents to be normal and healthy – not obsessive and deviant.

Clearly, Belmar had misread him. Clearly, Belmar had projected his own perversion. Clearly, Robert chose sides according to his own preference. Clearly...

"I've been dumped," he moaned miserably.

Once more, his thoughts traced the scant index of his known contacts. As a memory aid, he idly flipped through this same list in his telephone. Perusing each name, his recollections provided a face. An attitude. A demeanor. Then he mentally roleplayed the call.

"Hey, Blank, it's me. Toe. It's short for Roberto. Morales. Robert's friend. Right! That's me. Hello? Hello?"

"Oh, yeah," he breathed over that particular entry, "the potato salad incident." Last semester at the dorm's Halloween Block Party, Mister Blank had volunteered to fetch Robert a second helping of homemade potato salad. Roberto thought the offer a bit too forward and interested, so he had made an excuse to follow his supposed rival back to the banquet tables. There, he confronted the other about his saucy flirts, warning Mister Blank to "keep his pecker in his pants" and his potato salad spoon off Robert's plate.

Roberto told the third party, "Our buttholes are stamped 'export-only'."

That settled the matter. Of course, Mister Blank refused to speak to him since.

Next on the list. Another face and attitude drawn from memory. Another round of roleplay. Once he established the identity of this one, he keenly wished this Mister Blank would hang-up as fast as the first, since the second listing had a real problem with Roberto. More inter-personal jealousy.

Naturally, when he paused to be completely honest with himself, Roberto recognized a reversed polarity within the truth. *Perhaps*, he silently conceded, *I'm the problem in this case.*

Everybody screws up once. Maybe twice.

Because the next guy and the guy after that were part of the same misunderstanding. Unfortunately, were he to call either of those frat-brothers, both might show up to the appointed hour of rendezvous only to beat the living shit out of Roberto Morales. In fact, he deleted these entries along with another female entry, this being one of their fiancés. "She was a cracked bitch," he announced with a soft snarl.

So, on through the remainder of the list. Perhaps a hundred contacts, most of them high school and college acquaintanceships. Any one of them would immediately drop everything to rescue Bob Two in the same situation. None would come to the aid of Bob One.

He knew he could call Belmar. Boss would feel obligated to fetch him, but that ticket to ride seemed too costly. Their latest clash punctuated summer's end with a gigantic scarlet exclamation point, so he could never go back there. He deleted Belmar's contact information, too, lest the temptation return.

Only one name remained. "MOTHER". All caps.

As usual, she would blubber to hear his sad tale. Also, as usual, she would demand to know what he had done to Robert. He was such a nice young man. She wished the two of them would make friends and be happy.

Roberto suspected that she loved Robert more than he. Worse, he sometimes felt like she claimed him only to maintain access to the youth she had labeled as her 'second son'. If possible, she would probably swap their places without a thought and then she would quickly reject her only-born for a rabid pariah.

Yet she would also come for him. Three hours.

He refused to stoop so low. Not yet. Instead, he would continue walking northbound to improve the distance between himself and his scornful lover. *Former* lover.

"Who never really loved me," moaned Roberto.

A sudden fury of splashing, sloshing and slapping stopped him with a jerk. Spinning clockwise, his ears perked like radar dishes, he confronted the swamp, which now arched low over the two-lane like an emerald colonnade. Unseen for undergrowth and sluggish currents, two wild things struggled for existence. One dying. The other living for a while longer.

He shuddered. "Oh, man, this place is yucky-nasty-creepy. I really hate it and I *despise* snakes!"

Working the summer gig paid well, despite his personal prejudice. The internship also counted as credit, so he would shave several classroom hours and many thousands of dollars from his total tuition. Besides the vileness of the setting – and all that poop – fieldwork felt infinitely more dignified than most college-age employment. He pondered a hundred valid reasons to manhandle giant swamp serpents, despite the inevitable

Segment 14

sense of horror and disgust that accompanied each encounter.

Shoulders slumping again, Roberto noted a pregnant stillness, the contest having been won or lost, so he must wonder how long he had been standing and staring. Turning north, he stomped along the road, his pace timed to a hangdog march. His tread sluggish, broken and beaten. Tail tucked. Worm-eaten.

"Shut-up, you silly fool," he cursed himself. "You know why you volunteered for this shitty gig."

One reason, only. Robert Johnathan Price.

No matter his best intentions, the worst possible thing had happened. The one thing that he had worked so hard to avoid through years of torment in public schools and then three years of college. Somehow, somewhere, Robert Price had slipped off the hook.

By now, Robert would be swimming sparkling new waters, carefree and loose, and without Roberto's ever-watchful shadow hovering overhead. Anything could happen. In Belmar's company, *something* was bound to happen.

This proved to be Roberto's most putrid wound. Instinctively, from the earliest days of his memory, he had kept his friend close by exploiting his strangely rigid and religious understanding of the world.

Suffering this heretical bad thought about himself, Bob One physically shook his head to clear it. Then he slapped his face, either cheek, when this ideation returned but moments later.

Given Belmar's outspoken criticism, Roberto feared today would be the day. The last of so many things.

Blowing a long, releasing breath, he mentally raged to quiet the endless bickering and catcalls of his psychological menagerie. Into the hidden source of each snide, sniggering voice, he screamed promises of self-violence, this time uttering these too-familiar remarks as no idle threat.

Having been outed by Belmar's insensitive 'assistance', Roberto knew he could never recover his relationship with Robert. Not as they had been before.

His head brimmed with lies. Sexual propaganda.

"I swear," he threatened himself, "if you all don't shut-up this instant, I'm going to wade out into that swamp and feed myself to an alligator!"

Birds stopped squawking and insects fell silent. Only lifeless, watery sounds reached him from the gloom.

"That's better!" he insisted vehemently.

He continued marching, refusing to check his new phone for the time. He would call mom only when he could not stumble another step. Not a moment sooner.

As though marking his false bravado, a gust of warm, moist air bowled along the roadway corridor, sweeping bits of detritus along with it, so this matter curled and swirled between Roberto's knees. Overhead, scarcely visible for countless towering cypress crowns and secondary undergrowth, that vague sense of sunshine dimmed perceptibly. Though he expected the worst, Roberto hoped the weather would hold for the weekend.

Not for himself. Instead, he worried for...

"Shut-up! Shut-up! Shut-up!"

He stopped to pitch a tantrum, right there on the side of the road. He screamed. He stomped. He pinched slatted, hateful eyes to make a demented mask of his face. He clenched balled fists and he stood rigid still as though made of stone.

The honk of a horn jolted him a foot into the air. Somebody laughed.

Opening his eyes, Roberto watched a northbound truck surge around him. Through open windows, he heard its driver shouting. Something about the storm, heavy rains and flooding. All concluded with a resounding and clearly audible catcall. "Dumbass!"

The youth's stomach ground painfully. He bit a pouting lower lip.

Regardless of his twisted emotions, he thought he should call and warn his friend. If they offered a ride on their way out of the swamp, he would angrily refuse it. The first time. If they offered.

No answer. He tried again. No answer.

Biting his lower lip hard enough to draw blood – almost – his resolve collapsed. Searching through his inbound and outbound call logs, he found Belmar's number. This, he dialed without saving it into his contacts again.

Once more, he received no response. He tried again. A third time. He left a message.

Shrugging, he determined to go a bit further before he made another attempt. By now, he knew they had started walking their first transect of the day, which would require them to leave their electronics in the locked cab of Belmar's truck.

"Stupid shits!" he cursed.

Roberto had heard and seen the way his friend and Belmar talked about Crazy Cat Lady. She worried him much more than Belmar because she had the one thing that Robert had yet to understand. *Poontane.*

While he remained a virgin to heterosexual intercourse, Roberto instinctively knew his large friend must question the rest. In these questions resided doubt, wonder and a consequent potential for exploitation.

Segment 14

Roberto knew he required a single perfect moment to tip the balance. One instance of weakness and the proper setting could resolve *everything*.

Oh, the two of them were not without history. They had shared magically intimate moments from time to time. Confessed fantasies. Physical show and tell. A reciprocal exchange of grips. Mutual masturbation. Once.

Naturally, Roberto hoped for more. Much more.

Religion confused the man. Being an agnostic himself, Roberto understood the inherent conflicts attributable to remaining a celibate virgin within a profligate culture. The resulting frustration and desperate need produced rare moments of opportunity, which Bob One had progressively exploited since middle-school, hoping to broaden Robert's sexual horizons while steering him toward a particularly deviant constellation.

Lately, he felt a growing promise in their relationship. One more wine-soaked Saturday evening spent together in Robert's apartment...

He had been so close! Now, stomping along the often-patched roadway as thunderheads gathered overhead, Roberto feared he had lost all. No, he *knew* it was over. Finished.

When he traced that spiderweb of cause-and-effect, he first arrived at a familiar face. Belmar. Then he must push further, because he knew an interlude with the wildlife agent would only push Robert in the desired direction.

No, it's not Belmar. For the first time since he had noted formation of that odd triangle, Roberto recognized the true homewrecker among them. *Her.*

"She-demon!" he spat.

One sniff of Cat Lady's rotten flower would spell ruin for all, whether Belmar remained in the room or not. *Every bad thing must blossom from such spoiled buds.*

Segment 14

Through a dozen alleged 'girlfriends', Roberto had played the role of his friend's most trusted spiritual advisor. Each time Robert played 'stinky-pinky' and then pondered going farther, Roberto stepped forward to remind of vows and promises, wrapping all in bundles of righteousness and mortal sin. Religion proved to be a rich source of inspiration.

Too, he worked the opposite side of the equation with equal surety, pushing her away from Robert with the aid of boldfaced lies and judicious application of rumor or inuendo. Her. Always her. That nameless, omnipresent *her*.

Genesis taught the lure of an apple and a magical garden to the downfall of Eve, humankind's first hussy. Roberto knew better. The lure was no apple, and the garden grew tangled like the dark hair between Eve's thighs.

One sight. One taste. One touch.

Afterward, Robert would know. All doubts dispelled. Every question answered. Each smallest sexual detail, fallen into place.

Belmar had worked the situation adroitly. Roberto had used the same methods many times, himself. Insinuate, divide and then conquer.

So clever, the older man had somehow maneuvered Roberto into volunteering for such service. He had not shouted, "Get out!" Rather, he had goaded Roberto into leaving.

Tonight-.

Roberto's thoughts stopped within a brilliant flash of mental light. Something cold and heavy fell from a low overhang of Spanish moss. The momentous weight of it plunged him to the asphalt while stars filled his vision and vibrant lightning bolts erased his thoughts.

Stunned from the initial impact, he attempted to sit and right himself after his fall, but immediately experienced great distress in doing so. Something interfered with his every movement.

Worse, that incredible feeling of weight continued to mount. For a mad moment, Roberto thought perhaps an enormous length of heavy chain had plummeted through the treetops to continually pile on top of him. Perhaps dropped from an airplane or the international space station.

Its mass continued to compound itself. Crushing him. Relentlessly smashing his arms around his ribcage to compress his lungs and heart.

Recovering from the monster's initial assault, Roberto recognized his predicament in the mossy-green reticulations of a large constrictor. His fumbling fingers and flailing limbs quickly totaled the damage, so he found himself wrapped from ankle to neck.

Rearing above him while twisting into a perpendicular alignment with his bulging, blue-tinted face, the demon worm opened its pink-on-white mouth, spreading its wicked jaws to an impossible degree of separation. The beast squeezed and hissed. Its black eyes flinched through a studied measure of the young man's dimensions and worth.

In the next moment, Roberto's last pinched breath escaped with explosive force. He felt fangs raking his cheeks and shoulders, and he struggled alive through the first gulps of devour. Even as he felt swamp water rise around him. Then he suffocated and died.

After months of ravenous hunger, she had successfully tackled a large meal, crushing it lifeless within rolling coils. Thrashing amid vast swatches of roadside sawgrass, she worked her gaping mouth down around Roberto's head to his shoulders, where it alternated from right to left, frustrated and unable to engulf the man's entire torso with a single gulp.

While the body yet loomed warm against the swamp's cold, dark background, she surrendered her first deep-gulp. Instead, she determined to attempt the opposite approach, starting with Bob's feet. As before, she could swallow one leg or the other with ease. A bit of work fitted both booted feet into her throat, so she began swallowing his body to its knees and upper thighs. Once more, the young man's sizeable girth interrupted her efforts, so she hung, gagging, around his belted waist.

By the time she next choked away from her latest kill, the remains had cooled to ambient temperature and its extremities had seized with rigor. Too dark to see. Too stiff to manage. Too cold to devour.

Further spent and yet ravenous, the demon worm heaped herself into a frustrated ball beside Roberto's cooling corpse. Her engorged and heavily pregnant belly squirmed while her empty stomach churned, so her distended body warred with itself. From moment to moment, her primitive mind served the alternate biological causes of starvation and maternity.

Ultimately feeling portentously gravid, she uncoiled to slink away into a rising storm. Instinct would guide her suddenly urgent search for a dry, safe lair, and then she would hunt again.

SEGMENT 15

Sunday morning. The last day.

Bob Two sat atop the open tailgate of Belmar's pickup truck. He chewed the fingernails of his right hand down to the quick. Then he chewed cuticles.

Belmar approached from the north side of the east-west 'road' – this being really more of a muddy track – his arms swinging wide of his sludge-bound waddle. They had followed it off-road in 4x4 mode until even that capable machine could go no farther. While Two prepared for the day's work, Belmar had quickly shucked his boots to wade into the swamp, obviously tending a private errand. Now he returned with a strange swatch of material dangling from his right fist, its various loops dragging across the surface of the murky water. A wake of tangled waterlilies, waterhyacinth, waterlettuce, watergrass, hydrilla and a thousand other floating green things followed him back to shore.

Another day of mud and shit. Everything wet.

Bob Two sighed wearily. Watching Belmar climb a submerged, peat-heaped limestone ridge onto the motor track, he once more gloomily announced, "We should have gone back for him."

This being a monotonous ritual since Bob One had failed to arrive home the previous evening, Belmar blew a long, weary breath, shrugging and fumbling in the muck. He grunted his reply, "He's a grown man."

The wildlife agent must consciously caution himself to maintain use of the present tense. For Bob Two's sake, as much from a sense of liability, he repeatedly steered the responsibility back toward its origins. *What kind of moron throws a tantrum by attempting to walk out of the deep Everglades?*

By now, the kid had seen enough of the swamp to know both its bounty and its threat. To pontificate this never-ending struggle of the wilds, Belmar held forth his trophy.

"I spotted it from the roadway," he informed his younger intern, lifting a long, translucent ribbon to lay one of its ends on the crushed greenery beneath Two's dangling bare feet. Next, he spoke as he gently stretched the material to its length along the overgrown trail, saying, "This must feel really wonderful to the animal, since each scale comes apart so both its visible, upper aspects and its hidden, lower aspects peel away, shiny new and glossy smooth."

Bob Two's eyes continued to widen as he watched the man's display. A full yard across and forty-feet long!

"Of course, this being the case, we must take into account the fact that each scale is represented twice in the length and breadth of the shed. Once for the top of each scale and once for each scale's bottom. So, a sixty-foot shed skin like this comes from... what?"

"A thirty-foot-foot specimen."

"Right. Give or take." Rising from his task, having laid the shed cuticle atop the grass so its inside-out, milky-clear head poised to devour Bob Two, feet-first. Its tail disappeared along the weedy road, so-called. "Look at that girth. This girl is at least fourteen inches in diameter –

almost ten feet, all the way around! The biggest I've ever seen!"

When Bob Two pointed toward a kink in the display, Belmar sloshed through stunted sawgrass to remedy the error. Finished, he whistled, having added another six feet of actual length to the beast.

"That's more than ten-yards of snake," he huffed, hauling himself onto the tailgate to sit beside his youthful aide.

There, he pondered the promise and foreboding of the day. Overhead, a drear gray sky rumbled, its expanse further dimmed by an endless sprawl of towering cypress crowns. Turning a squinted gaze on the heavens, Belmar sucked a sour tongue.

"It's too much for two," he ultimately admitted, "but we can't go home like this."

"His mom is throwing a fit, you know," informed Bob Two. As he spoke, he silenced the muffled buzz of his telephone by pressing its buttons through the pocket of his khaki shorts. "You don't know her as well as I do."

"I got to know Bob One better than I liked," affirmed Belmar, "so I can guess."

"Something happened to him."

"Yeah, it's called a temper tantrum."

"We shouldn't have stayed at her place last night," gushed an obviously guilt-ridden Bob Two, "doing what we were doing."

Belmar's grin slanted lecherously. He slapped Bob's thigh to make the young man jump, so Bob leapt off the tailgate into the grass, barefoot and cursing.

"You seemed to enjoy the fun," he scolded the kid. "Besides, we had nothing to do with Two's choice, and *you* said we shouldn't go after him."

"Great. It's all my fault."

"I didn't say that!"

"But it is, and you know it!" Bob's shoulders slumped. Brooding angrily, he kicked a hunk of rotted cypress into the water, where its mass landed with a gelatinous plop. "I'm his friend. Not you. I should have stuck up for him."

"Sure, you should have done, and you did. You made the best choice you could, given circumstance. Plus, I never heard you say anything bad about the boy." Belmar thought a moment longer. "Except to call him a 'scorned woman', which I think is apt."

Two's face darkened with the overcast skies. He scowled, his gaze scanning the claustrophobic horizon without seeing a thing. As any worthy southern man might do, he tucked his hands into his back pockets, so his palms gripped his ass cheeks. He rocked on anxious heels. Thinking.

"We should have gone back for him."

Sighing wearily and feeling the spin of mud-mired wheels in his brain, Belmar lay backward into the bed of his truck to clasp his hands behind his head. The boy's worried mother had called just before sunrise that morning, jolting him out of Cat Lady's disorderly bed, which slept three at the time. From that moment, he had felt a sinking, burning sensation in his guts. Naturally, he had been measuring oblique legal angles since.

"You said he'd done this before," asserted Belmar, speaking to watery heavens, his eyes closed contemplatively. "Run off after a fit, I mean."

Bob blew a long, frustrated breath, which he had apparently held compressed behind tightly pursed lips. "Yes, Belmar, he does this often, as I already told you a hundred times."

"So? What's one more?"

Segment 15

"Like I said, he calls his mother the way most people brush their teeth. Morning, noon and night." The kid turned to approach the inverted snake's head, now empty, and there he crouched to examine its sinister portent in close detail. "When she calls, he always answers if he can. Always. His momma-complex drives me nuts, since I never saw a shorter leash tied around anyone's neck."

Belmar shrugged. "Last night was... unusual."

Rolling his eyes behind slatted lids, Bob relived the disgrace and ecstasy of the evening. Every part of his body tingled wickedly. Whispering softly to himself, he breathed, "The worm has turned."

Boss grunted impatiently, "What's that you say?"

"I said," Bob Two returned more assertively, "last night changed many things, but it didn't relieve me of my responsibility."

"You're not the boy's daddy," reminded Belmar.

"Yet I am my brother's keeper," counter-minded Bob Two. When his older companion groaned miserably to hear him paraphrase biblical mumbo-jumbo, Bob regretted this imitation of his father, 'Big John the Baptist'. He attempted to cover by appending, "Look, we have to do something. If we don't tell his mom what's going on, she'll call the Coast Guard, and you can believe that."

Belmar sat upright. "Don't tell me."

Turning in his squat, Bob squinted his eyes against the general glow of sunrise, answering, "Yeah. She's done it before. Twice."

"The United States Coast Guard?" *Is there another?*

"And a couple of sheriff's offices," grumped Bob, rising again to kick the grotesque molt back into its swampy home, "state and local police, too, of course." Then he further added, "and that's only the two times he went 'missing' near water." He formed quotations with the

Segment 15

two forefingers of either hand. "I can't count the number of times that she sent local cops looking for him back home. Scores, at least."

Belmar's face paled. His stomach churned acid.

"Shit."

"Yeah," breathed Bob Two, verged on tears, "shit."

Turning the holler's circumference, Belmar surveyed droops of Spanish moss that dangled from every cypress limb down to head-height above the track. A hundred yards west, they had turned off the splintered two-lane to follow this trail into the bush to its head in this dome-like void of undergrowth. Brackish water and lush swampland surrounded the low ridge on all sides. Upon arrival, he had immediately spotted the shed skin twisted into lower limbs of a stunted bald cypress.

This much Bob Two knew. Belmar had deliberately failed to identify countless scraps of perhaps a hundred other molts. He attempted to twist his expertise into a plausible story that attributed all that activity to a hundred individual serpents, each having staked this particular holler for home turf.

Yet, no matter the chosen angle of perspective, he could not fit this incongruous picture into frame. So, he must confess the truth if only to himself.

"It's one big mother," murmured Bob Two, as though reading his mentor's thoughts.

"Right." Belmar spoke timorously, fully concerned.

Musing silently through several pregnant seconds, which the sky filled with rumbles of distant thunder, Two added, "It's a recent molt." Belmar nodded. Two next asserted, "Being so large, she must be gravid."

"Heavily so."

"She'll be hungry."

"Ravenous."

Segment 15

This line of reasoning could resolve many points of order. An unusual quietude noticeable within surrounding 'Glades. A depressed representation of large mammals in his scat surveys. A reduced presence of avians hunting its waterways. A general absence of crocodilians there, too. These skin sheds. Bob One's mysterious disappearance.

"Thirteen," Belmar soberly and enigmatically announced aloud.

Pondering an instant profusion of possibilities, Bob Two dully asked, "Thirteen-what?"

"Cats." Belmar gushed, pushing himself off the truck's tailgate while fetching a bundle of keys from his right front pocket. These, he applied to a large toolbox bolted to the front of its bed. Opening this wide to rummage within its contents, he said, "Cass only counted thirteen strays yesterday."

"So?"

"She counted three times as many only days earlier."

Bob One opened his mouth to speak too quickly and, no doubt, make another statement of stupidity. Instead, he bit his lower lip. He thought long and hard, if only to benefit his missing friend.

"If she's hunting housecats," guessed Bob, "she must be scraping the bottom of the barrel."

"Right." Belmar retrieved a short-barreled pump shotgun from the toolbox, offering this to his young protégé, who accepted it with obvious reluctance. Extracting a second riot gun, he anticipated Bob's line of thought, teaching, "I think she's worked herself into a bit of a hole, here. Back home amidst the Amazonian rain forests, her kind lives in an aquatic environment that's in a constant state of flux, alternately flooding and receding. Her kind grew fat by lazily hanging from the trees to await delivery of their next meal as it came swimming along the current. If she should hunt an area to emptiness, she could just drop into that same current and let it carry her effortlessly to the next fertile hunting ground."

Next, Belmar withdrew a pair of webbed vests and several boxes of shotgun shells, tossing the former onto the tailgate and then handing the latter to his fumbling assistant. Making an obvious double-check of their needs, he verified his belt for the presence of pistol and spare mags, nodding to himself.

Indicating that Bob should accompany him to the tailgate and then imitate his loading of the weapon, Belmar continued his grim lesson. He spoke slowly and deliberately to walk a razor's edge of information as cut by the division of too-much from too-little.

"Sure, the 'Glades flood," he mused, smashing open a box of shells, which he started jacking into the riot gun's empty breech, "but on a completely different schedule and in a totally different way. Being a river sixty-miles wide, this swamp never moves quickly – certainly not fast enough to continually feed a giant snake grown too pregnant to swim away."

Bob also smashed a box of shells. He also began pushing one round after another into the shotgun's lock, though his performance seemed most awkward in comparison.

"Our baby grew fat while eating all the deer, wild hogs and gators in this basin," he quipped, referring to the green anaconda that he suspected of having eaten their friend, too, "and then she got knocked up, no doubt expecting an Amazonian bounty to simply come drifting past her flooded lair as she brooded."

Segment 15

"Instead," growled Bob through gritted teeth as his fingers fumbled to feed the shotgun's full magazine, "she finds herself living in a veritable desert."

"And only stray cats to eat."

Surrendering the task when Belmar signaled that he should do so, he continued to imitate the man's handling of his shotgun. When he struggled, Belmar quickly reviewed operation of the firearm, showing the younger man how to 'safe' and 'arm' the weapon, how to carry it, how to fire and reload it, and finally, how to avoid shooting either of them by accident. All reminders of formal training that the kid had forgotten from summer's glorious start.

"Since you're inexperienced, you keep your chamber empty and your weapon safed. If and when I call your name, only then should you rack the slide to load a round. Got it? And, Bob? Don't point it above the ground or below the treeline unless you intend to kill something. Understand?"

Bob bit his lower lip. He nodded. Uncertainly.

Waxing serious, Belmar strapped his gear onto his body, including a webbed cross-braces to hold spare ammo in pouches, a utility knife, a pair of flashlights and a small first-aid pouch with snake-bite kits. Stuffing its pouches with spare shotgun shells, they cleaned the truckbed, tossing crumpled boxes and wrappers into a small pile of beer cans collected against one of its cab-side corners.

Slinging their weapons over shoulders, both men turned to confront their destination. The holler steamed silently, and only insects dared to break the tableau by darting and flitting through dim, slanted sunbeams. Overhead, cypress crowns danced in a rising wind, while higher still a fleece of black thunderheads approached from the southeast, these the angry remnants of a massive tropical storm that had died over Miami a week earlier.

Segment 15

Bob Two's phone started buzzing again, reminding them to stow their electronics before plunging into chest-deep waters. Fishing this device from his pocket, Bob silently questioned boss.

"Answer it," instructed Belmar, "and tell her the kid dropped his phone again. Tell her he's fine and working the far end of a transect. Too far, in fact, to pass the call."

"She'll want to speak to him."

Belmar's face clouded darker than the unseen sky. He pursed frustrated lips.

"Hello, Missus Morales," answered Bob. Then he told Belmar's lies.

When she insisted, the older man leaned into the conversation, too loudly saying, "Your son is a fully grown man, Missus Morales. He'll call you when he can call you. Until then, stop pestering us, we have work to do!" Then he savagely motioned for Bob to disconnect and lock the phone away.

Miserably, the younger man complied, promising to have Roberto call his anxious mother at the first available moment. He concluded the call by sheepishly repeating, "Yes, ma'am. I know he's still your baby-boy. I understand. Yes, ma'am. Belmar is a jerk. Yes, ma'am...."

Finally, she let him go with an unhappy clatter of her dentures. Bob Two disconnected, grimacing. Yet, he felt somehow relieved to lock his phone in the glove compartment of Belmar's truck. For a few hours, at least, its absence promised peace and quiet if not peace-of-mind.

As he rejoined Belmar at the edge of the swamp, the older man said, "Your pal is fine, Bob. I'm sure of that much."

"How do you know?"

Segment 15

The man shrugged, stepping off the soggy bank to instantly plunge thigh-deep in muck and mud. Everything grew green atop the land and the water, both, so they must push through a swirling, rolling chocolate soup topped by a frothy green foam.

"We app-tracked his phone to this bit of the highway, where it went silent. So, we know he made it this far."

"That's what worries me most," gloomed Bob Two, since he must lift both arms high to keep his shotgun dry.

"Look, kid, I know these people. I grew-up here, remember? With that storm approaching, nobody would pass a kid walking along these low roads without stopping to offer a ride."

"You're sure about that, are you?"

Tipping his head to concede, Belmar grunted to waddle through waist-deep shallows, his feet buried in muck above his ankles. "Most of them, anyway. Sure, a few of the clownier sort might pelt him with empty beer cans, but somebody would stop to give him a lift. Eventually. At least as far as the next corner store."

Bob stewed silently for a while since he must struggle to breathe for the weight of soupy water. Then he stated the obvious. "Even if the passenger turned out to be Roberto? *Our* Roberto?"

After a short ponder, Belmar nodded. "Even for Roberto. Hell, maybe *especially* for Roberto since he stands out in these parts like a booger on a wineglass. Anybody would take pity on such an ignorant young fool found marching through the 'Glades unarmed – and with a flood approaching, to boot."

Craning his neck to survey unseen skies, Bob's gloom only deepened, descending atop his shoulders with all the dread weight of low-hanging creepers. Two studied

Segment 15

his host's assertions, but quickly found them wanting. Mostly due to his familiarity with Roberto's stubborn pride. Despite the dangers, he doubted his friend would seek or accept a ride from such people. He knew too well how that kind managed his kind. More, he had long accepted the irrationality of Roberto's perverse sense of self.

Robert knew, of course. He had always known.

Same as he knew he could never talk Belmar into ending the hunt prematurely, since the older man needed cash so badly. Still, Bob Two suffered the gnaw of a guilty conscience and he could not so readily dismiss his friend's untimely disappearance.

Once more, he cursed himself for a traitor, repeating, "We should have gone back for him."

SEGMENT 16

Most everybody visited Bailey's Corner Store before the onset of a large storm. Swamp people knew how to live well amid a land forever drowning. A bit of extra dew would not dampen their understanding.

Yet few failed to anticipate flooded byways and inaccessible homesteads. Too, the power regularly failed, which limited a home's access to freshwater wells and power for entertainment systems. So, every citizen of account kept a few working generators and a sizeable reserve of fuel on hand.

Since the entire forest stood inside a single river that stretched to the coast at a width of up to sixty miles, even a vast amount of rainfall would do small damage to the natural wilds of the park and its more populated surrounds. The deluge might drown the roads for a few days at a time, but the sluggish current rarely washed anything away. Perhaps as a means of compensating for its many hardships, the swamp's festering stifle returned at least this small measure of safety and shelter as reward to its loyal denizens.

Sunday afternoon, perhaps a half-hour before first rain, Sam Dell stood before Bailey's much-abused counter, his face pale and his eyes wide. Shockingly void of emotion, the man flatly informed his old acquaintance, "It ate Jenny last week."

Beyond the store's ad-plastered plate-glass windows, surrounding undergrowth had finally come alive to dance before a gusting wind. Wetter than lower-lying air, a humid downdraft rolled into the crossroads hollow to pour across overgrown waters and chase detritus along weathered surfaces of both roadways. Daylight darkened perceptibly yet again, one of many progressive dimming events that marked arrival of denser and denser thunderheads.

By now, though the clock marked early afternoon, the day had darkened to half-night. Scant traffic rushed home behind glaring headlamps.

Bailey measured Sam up and down, searching for signs of sobriety or drunkenness. Ultimately, he determined the man to be sober, so he sat taller atop his groaning stool to prompt, "Is that so?" As any worthy southern boy might do, regardless of company.

"It's the honest-to-god truth, Bailey Matchlock, and I swear it so."

"Good enough, then, Sam Dell, and that's a damned shame. Really, it's just awful... but you're sure it weren't no gator?"

Sam frowned unhappily. "Have you seen a big gator, lately? I remember when you couldn't get to church of a Sunday morning for having to run them off the blacktop by the dozens. Big ones and little ones, too. Now, I can't remember the last time I saw a large reptile of any kind skittering around these parts. Can you?"

Bailey chewed his tongue. Having already processed the man's purchase of whiskey, he simply waited for his guest to leave, filling the air in between with words.

"I can't say so, myself, Sam, but it's been a while."

"I called the wildlife guys," continued the village pariah – this being on account of his having killed his own best friend to steal the man's wife, "I guess you heard about that."

"Oh, yeah, we've been talking. They tell some tall tales, I guess."

"Have you seen them today?"

Bailey shook his head. "Can't say that I have. Not today. Yesterday, maybe. No, it was Friday. They intended to count poop and play barefoot games with scaly monsters. None of it made much sense to me."

Then the proprietor felt a tingle down below, which eventually surfaced in his brain as bad thoughts. Small-town folk will often suffer such, when in the company of the lowest rung.

Mischievously, he said, "I don't suppose you checked over to Cassie's place, did you? From what I understand, that wildlife fellah has been spending a great deal of time out that way." When he saw how Sam's face drained a paler shade, he slyly added, "But I guess you already know all about that, Sam, living only yards away from her, as you do."

Though he half-expected an angry exhibition, Sam held his own counsel until his face returned from an alabaster dearth to a rosy flush. Gripping two balled fists around the brown-paper sack that wrapped his fifth, Sam sucked a sour tongue, his lips silently writhing.

Ultimately, he replied, "Yeah. I guess she did mention something about that, a while back."

"She did?" marveled a skeptical store proprietor. "Hell, Sam, the way Cat Lady tells the same story, she wouldn't piss on your head if your hair caught fire, and she for damned sure wouldn't speak to you, face-to-face. Yet, you claim she told you so. A while back. Hmm."

Too hotly, Sam rejoined, "She did so!" He sounded defensive. Petulant and petty and defensive. "It was a few days back, she-." He stopped himself, biting his lower lip again.

"Oh, yeah," mused Bailey as he feigned the recovery of some profound artifact, "I suppose that was the fuss we all heard a few nights back, just as you claim. For the longest while, nobody could say what happened, exactly, but now I hear you marking yet another epic row with Cat Lady Cass. So, I guess that's the deal, after all."

Shaking his head, Bailey reached for a rumpled magazine, which he used to fan himself. Waxing diplomatic once more, he grinned into Sam's angry glower.

"Say," he poked, "why'd you come back to the 'Glades this time, Sam? Did you run out of money or love over to Tampa way? Same as happened in Charlotte and Atlanta and, ah, where'd you run to hide before that? I forget."

The man's brows knitted more tightly. His scowl improved enormously, so Sam appeared to ponder inky black thoughts of murder and mayhem.

Of course, Bailey knew Sam to be capable of such crimes, since he had been a vocal member of the gossip-jury that had accused, tried and convicted the man. Everyone knew Sam had killed Lonnie "Lon" Seminole some thirty years earlier. So, he would not make the mistake of both teasing Sam Dell and turning his back to him. Rather, Bailey drew comfort from his closely concealed shotgun and the generous self-defense laws of Southern Florida. More than one felon had started his sentence while healing from Bailey's deadly aim.

According to his self-confidence then, he prodded. He poked. Wondrous, he asked, "Do *you* even know why you came back this time?"

Sam chewed that sour tongue. His fingers traced the bottle's cap through its paper wrapper. Dread and longing warred for space behind the regret-fogged lenses of his dark eyes.

"After all these years? After all you done?"

Ultimately, as though he might still somehow recover his reputation among disaffected neighbors, Sam asserted, "I did nothing wrong. Not what you all think I did, anyway."

Bailey snapped the fingers of his free hand. He fanned himself while rolling his eyes, his memory filled by new and improving knowledge.

"Oh, that's right. They didn't convict you for the murder of your best friend – which is clearly not something the local football hero would do – no, they convicted you of a lesser crime, as I recall. What was it, now? Lying and cheating?"

"Obstruction of justice."

Snapping his fingers again, the pudgy clerk acknowledged this truth with a happy waggle of his jowls. "That's right! What do they call it, now a'days? Scientifically, I mean? Oh, yeah. 'Horny stupidity'."

With passage of his final ominous insult, a worldwide sheet of lightning spread across the entire sky above Okeechobee and the 'Glades. Deafening and immediate, a skull-crushing peal of thunder followed. Both men jumped with a start.

Into the echoes ringing within their skulls, Sam stiffly insisted, "I know what you all think of me, Bailey Matchlock. I ain't no moron though!"

"That so?" Bailey abruptly stopped fanning himself to lean forward off his stool and loom large in the center of Sam's burning gaze, so he presented the full menace of his paunchy yet sizeable bulk. "Then what do you call a man who murders his lover's husband – his own *best friend* – in cold blood? Hmm? You'd hang on that man a sign for genius, would you?"

Sam chewed his tongue a moment longer. Then, gripping his brown paper sack like a talisman, he spun on his right heel to leave, neck and ears burning violently.

When the door chime rang the man's good-bye, Bailey grinned broadly and waved toodle-oo-style with five fat fingers. "Y'all come back now! Y'hear?"

Stomping to his truck, which he had left parked alongside the store's gas pumps, Sam cursed Bailey Matchlock and all his small-town cronies. He loved and hated them, if only because he longed to belong and knew he that he could not.

Bailey asked why Sam had returned, but Sam thought the answer should seem obvious since he always left for the same reason, too. *Them.* All of them. *They* were the reason that he had returned home again, if only because an aging town pariah could not die unknown.

Like a cursed pension, Sam's reward of infamy and notoriety had proved to be eternal. Forever. A vast, immortal sum of guilt and blame that could never be spent, squandered or gambled away during his lifetime. Rather, he must discharge this final debt with the explosive belch of his last breath.

Even so, his family name would linger in shameful arrears among village ledgers, its scarlet letters and numerals etched in blood and not a damned thing he could do to balance his books. Suffering a fateful insight, Sam gritted regretful teeth.

Even if Tallahassee charged a different crime, every inhabitant of their tiny village knew a better and more certain truth. Worse yet, the courts of village opinion offered no bar of appeals. Only the same body of judges could un-render their own verdicts, and this they would never do.

Somehow, he had hoped to convince them of the truth. Once – long ago – he wished he could make them believe that he was, at worst, an adulterer. Never a murderer of any kind, but especially not the slayer of his childhood friend.

So, when Sam's daddy had died, he returned home for the last time. To tend the funeral and pay last respects. Never to linger. Never to stay.

Again, he had failed. Utterly.

His father's snide voice told him so. Sam hated himself, accordingly. Slumping miserably, he finished fueling his father's truck, which he then drove seven miles south to his father's house, where he began drinking in his father's porch swing.

Nothing his own. All his father's and grandfather's. Everything used. Secondhand. Patched and mended. Rusted or corroded. Rotting. Slow, by inches and degrees. The way mildew climbs a whitewashed wall, season upon season, its decay and ruin a timeless, motionless thing that yet succeeds in pulling every human notion back down into the muck and mud of its origins.

This, the same filth that had spawned humankind, too. Perhaps this one base quality of the swamp more than any other brought its devoted sycophants back home again and again, no matter how far or how long they might stray.

While they mistakenly knew him for a murderer, the people here knew him, all the same. As one of their own. No matter how marked he might be, they must claim him as kin or neighbor. *Isn't that the definition of 'home'?*

A beaten dog having run off to sulk in the wilderness, he had returned to this murky berg a dozen times through the last thirty-five years. Tail-tucked, ears-pinned and trembling each time, he always came simpering back to lick nervous lips and manage heaving bowels. Terrified, but desperately so.

    Atlanta. Charlotte. Dallas.

    All places he had known. All soils where he had struggled to take root. All cold memories within his mind. Each a tumble of lost and lonely days that merely marked the torn calendar of a reformed felon.

    No helping hands. No pointing fingers, either.

    He could never decide which seemed worse. When he lived out there, he pined for home, and visa-versa. Out there, nobody knew him for a murderer – then again, nobody knew him at all. Here, at least, nobody must be told his name since everyone shared gossip about the town's only damned killer.

    As he turned onto his weedy drive, rain began falling in thick, heavy drops. Or, perhaps more likely, rain had been falling for some time, only managing to reach his windshield when he drove into the claustrophobic holler that sheltered his ancestral homestead.

    Habitually, he looked for Jenny, expecting her to come bounding down the steps to charge the truck for her usual treat – a miniature pecan pie purchased from Bailey's larder. Heavily, he accepted the terrible truth of her frightening disappearance, and he felt *old*. Ancient. Near death.

    Like a vast, rolling stone, he felt the future bearing down upon him to make its last pinch before it squashed him flat. From middle age, he had noticed its approach – every day a bit closer – but its pending collapse now loomed large overhead. Lately, the measured gap between life and death left small space for joy and no room at all for the start of something new.

Segment 16

Sorrowfully, his lips trembling sloppily though he had yet to take a drink, he bemoaned his lot. Never again would he establish another human relationship with either human or beast. Cass had long ago rejected him, no matter his self-deceptions, and he no longer kept the strength or patience to train a new pup.

His truck slid to a moribund halt in the rain-stirred mud of his driveway. For a time, he sat in the silence of a killed motor, his thoughts dominated by sounds of fat raindrops pelting across its cabin. Nothing more. No desires. No wishes. No hopes.

Dully, he stared at his empty porch, which held an empty chair that no longer sheltered his canine companion in his absence. If daddy's house had been a drear place before, at least he once had Jenny to welcome him home. Now the darkness behind its windows seemed blacker. Emptier. Scarier.

Anything might have happened while he was away. Anyone might be waiting for him inside.

Then he chided himself for a worry-worn fool. Lon Seminole had no family outside Sam and *her*. His mother died shortly after he graduated high school, and his father had been absent too long to remember. No aunts. No uncles. An only child. So, no one would avenge him.

Sam Dell slept safe, even if he rarely slept well. *Decades*, he pondered morosely. Wasted and restless. Never a place to call home. Never another friend. Another woman.

Sam died with Lon, on his knees. Bleeding.

His love-life died the same way. By *her* hand. On its knees. Bleeding. Still. Decades later.

Sitting in his truck's cab, watching rain sheet his forward windshield to erase the shitiness of everything, Sam pealed a paper sack from the bottle's neck to spin its cap loose. Tipping his head to bob his throat, he drank one long, deep drink. Then he capped his poison again, vowing to resist further temptation.

"Tonight," he whispered harshly, "I'm going to do it. Really do it. Under cover of this storm. I'll sneak along the back trail to her porch, and then I'll kick in her front door to a roar of thunder. After that, the devil may care what follows, but I won't!"

Despite his bitter resolve, he thoughtlessly spun the cap to drink again. Again, he vowed this temptation would be the last.

"Afterward, I'll shoot myself in the mouth, Jen," he announced with a voice slurred by drink poured into an empty stomach. "That's the best way to go."

When he ultimately realized a terrible new truth about himself, he spun the cap a third time. This, he knew, must be the *true* reason for his return.

Her. *Ever for her.*

SEGMENT 17

Sheet lightning. Gusting wind. Torrents of rain.

Belmar and Bob Two huddled on Cat Lady's porch, soaked so thoroughly that the downpour had washed most of the mud and watergrass from their clothes and boots. Again, the older man knocked, his fist making a thunder of the rattling door frame to compete with the rumbles of god-games as played high above their mortal heads.

Presently, a porch light ignited to blind them. The door snapped open. A shotgun barrel pushed through the gap, aimed for Belmar's testicles through the yet locked screen.

"Cass, it's us! Let us inside!" shouted the wildlife agent, jumping in fright. Afterward, his demeanor drooped like that of a wet cat.

"What the hell for?" she wondered sleepily. "Have you come to kill me?"

That snapped their heads. The two of them exchanged puzzled glances. Had they, or had they not, spent the previous evening plugging all her holes at the same time in a mutually desperate attempt to make her aged body completely airtight?

Bob resisted the urge to shift himself. Belmar seemed more inclined to the obvious side of human nature.

Gripping himself with an obscene chuckle, he gawked. "You're not serious! Come on! Invite us inside!"

Crazy Cat Lady squinted suspiciously into the glare of her porch light. She scratched her upper right thigh through a lacy night-thing and clearly nothing more.

This time, Bob could not resist the urge. It sometimes hurt when it caught in his underwear where the elastic band wrapped around his leg.

"We did that last night," she reminded harshly. "I'm sore. Worn out. Come back next weekend."

She slammed the door. Sheet lightning crossed the cosmos with a brilliance that momentarily blinded. Then the inherent thunder of its passage immediately deafened them.

As revealed by that strobe-light flash, the swamp stirred a sodden frenzy, everything moving and swaying and yielding to the wind and the rain. The water churned beneath a spiky fur of skyfall, and a normally sluggish current surged through the glades' tangled roots.

Undeterred, Belmar banged again. "You don't understand, you crazy bitch! We didn't come to come! The roads are awash! We have nowhere else to go!"

"Get along to Sam Dell's place, then," she screeched through her closed front door. "He's your best friend these days. Ain't he?"

"I don't even know that loser. Come on, Cass!"

Belmar continued to bang and bang and bang on the locked screen door. When he wrenched it off its hinges, the main house door snapped open a crack. That impossibly wide barrel protruded.

Bob Two ducked aside. Belmar dropped to a crouch.

BOOM! CHICK-CHUCK! BOOM! CHICK-CHUCK! BOOM! CHICK-CHUCK!

She fired and reloaded three times. Belmar stood, enraged, and then he kicked her front door inward,

Segment 17

splintering its jamb and fracturing the frame that held its hinges. Smashing into Cassie's startled face, the force of this blow knocked her backward, arms pinwheeling.

Her shotgun landed on the couch. Her body skidded through the front parlor into her kitchen.

Belmar followed. As best he could manage, Bob Two closed the door after them, quieting the sounds of natural rage as prospered outside while emphasizing its more human variety within. Cat Lady screeched for them to leave her house. Belmar repeatedly called her a crazy bitch to include every colorful variation on the theme as expressed in English and Spanish epithets and curses.

Once she leapt to her feet, ready to fight, Belmar gripped her arms. She preceded to kick and bite. He pinned her to the couch atop her smoking shotgun. They struggled violently.

Bob Two retreated to her bathroom to fetch a pair of towels. Before he returned, he stripped naked, showered and dried.

When he reappeared in the living room, he found Belmar sitting on top of Cat Lady's chest, both of them winded and exhausted by their struggles. Angrily, his boss confronted him.

"Where in hell were you?"

Bob Two tossed him a towel. "Showering." He had deliberately wrapped the second around his muscular waist, an enormous erection making a teepee of the material just below his navel.

That set them both up peaceably enough. Once she surrendered, Belmar pushed backward, stood, and then heaved away to expend the rest of Cassie's limited hot water supply.

Accepting an offered tissue, she sat straight to wipe blood from beneath her nose, an obvious result of the kicked-in door. While she tended herself, she warily watched Bob move around the room. She need not marvel at the size of his interest since she had already come to know him with an intimate familiarity.

Abrasive as always, she ultimately asked, "Did you find your lost friend? Or should I call him your lost lover?"

Bob sighed restlessly, admiring the drum of rainfall and the tympany of thunder. That luminous pop.

He sat in her recliner, opposite her couch. He crossed legs, allowing the towel to fall away. To encourage her continued fascination, he occasionally paused to stroke himself stiff. She admired the pink-on-purple swell of him, licking her lips to pontificate.

"Oh," Bob Two sighed again, "he's dead. I'm sure of it now."

Nonplussed, Cass rearranged the cushions of her sofa, grimacing at the damp and mud. Wiping at this with Bob's towel when he tossed it, she made a bigger mess of things before she finally made way there. Bob admired the naked flex of her aged yet firm muscles. Not an ounce of fat to be seen.

Small breasts. Minimal yet sufficient arms and legs. Beefy thighs. A stringy ass, really, but Bob attributed this to her age. For fifty-something, she smoked!

Noticing his interest, Cass returned to the sofa to sit, unashamed to spread her legs comfortably. He stroked himself and watched. She flexed her right leg open and shut, open and shut, a sort of nervous tic.

"Pervert," she hissed hatefully. "I'm old enough to be your mother. Why do you keep coming around?"

"Why do you keep opening the door?"

"I didn't! You two kicked it in, remember!"

"Did we?" Bob stroked himself before a slanted, arrogant grin. "Maybe you want something different tonight. Something rougher."

She smirked. Her leg jogged back and forth, back and forth. The hairy tangle of her flashed open and shut. Pink and gray. Pink and gray.

So furry. Retro, they called it. 'Seventies-style.

"You don't shave."

"Only my armpits and legs, junior," she returned with abundant hostility. "Let me guess. Like your juvenile-oriented boss, you also have mommy issues."

He returned her smirk. He paused to keep himself stiff with a few quick rubs.

"I suppose I must. I know I want you again. No matter what else happens tonight."

For some reason, this opened her eyes. She sat straighter. She licked her lips. He right leg hung wide. Opened.

"Really?"

He nodded. He settled backwards in the easy chair, so his knees spread wider, too. Starting from a giant pair of ripe, swollen balls, an enormous stalk of a penis lay across his belly, stiffening and swelling larger and larger by the moment. Cass licked wanton lips, though she instantly regretted this weakness.

Then she found her right forefinger had strayed into her own personal wetness. It wiggled and she tingled accordingly. Delightfully.

Sounds of a rushing shower fell still. The storm filled a thrilled silence. The two of them watched each other masturbate with an intermittent application of their individual right hands.

Again, abrasive as always, though her voice choked huskily, Cass acidly demanded, "I guess you two are butt-buddies together."

Bob tipped his head. He opened his mouth to refute her assertion, but then thought better of it. Instead, he said nothing. His right two forefingers worked with his thumb to make his purpled member swell to enormous proportions. He knew she wanted to gnaw on the fleshy mushroom of his head.

When he refused to debunk or affirm her assertion, she once more licked lustful lips. Somewhat more desperately than she liked, the older woman asked, "What are the odds that I'll get to see something... special?"

Grinning lecherously, he asked what she wanted to see. Belmar finished his shower. They heard the stall door slam open and then immediately closed again.

"You two. Together."

His grin broadened impossibly. He tipped an acquiescent head, allowing, "That leaves room for enormous possibilities. Maybe you should be more specific."

"I want to rub you both against each other while I use my mouth on you."

Bob's testicles stirred wondrously within his bunched scrotum. He leaked.

Belmar exited her bathroom in time to hear the second half of her request, "And then I want to help you both suck each other."

"No anal?" queried Belmar, drying his hair.

She shook her head, turning her body atop the sofa to make certain he could see the busy wiggle of her right forefingers. "Not this time."

Entering the living room, he finished drying himself. Pointedly, he drew the towel around his middle-aged paunch, which remained respectably diminutive and marbled, and then he draped the terrycloth over a standing lamp, muffling its glow.

"What do you say, Bob Two? Should we give the little lady what she wants?"

Bob nodded. He moved forward to sit on the edge of the easy chair's ample lap, jutting stiffly forward.

Squirming backward into the cushions as though fearful of her beaus, Cat Lady deliberately made it wetter. Falsely fearful, she purred, "Animals like you normally tie a girl down before they molest her. Don't they?"

Belmar manipulated himself, proud of his girth if not his length, the former being an easy match for his young friend, while the latter left a bit to desire in comparison. No matter, thought Belmar, since his would get more backdoor action than that monster ever could!

Bob Two stood to remove a pair of cords from the nearest set of curtains. These he snapped into a twisted promise of knots and restraint. The two men approached their squirming quarry, everything stiff, pink and swollen.

Like a pack of ravenous wolves, Belmar and Bob leapt across the intervening distance, the former pinning Cassie's wiry legs while Bob Two held her torso and arms. Together, they tied her to the couch in a most graphic and vulnerable pose, so every limb splayed and all her holes gaped readily.

For the first two hours, they took what they wanted from her, utterly selfish and violent in their need. Once they initially spent themselves, Cass started to work on their perversions with a hussy's will. By the time the storm crossed midnight, she had them in each other's mouths and more.

Bob Two never came so hard in his life. Belmar and Cass simply enjoyed a rare but not entirely uncommon treat. Throughout the course of their extended bout of debauchery, lightning flashed the sordid scenery like lurid flashbulbs.

    Her eyes rolling to delirious whites, Cat Lady screamed deep into the night. Thunderclaps scarcely muffled their sexual din.

SEGMENT 18

Sam crouched on his neighbor's porch, mentally torn and twisted. He watched the fun with wide eyes, but he could not choose rage over excitement. Both emotions entwined within the mixing vessel of his guts, so anger churned against lust in a wild, primitive way.

He wanted to join them. He wanted to kill them.

Her. Belmar. And that kid, what's-his-name. Both men violently abusing her at the same time. Her body lithe and athletic, fully tanned and uncut, she wildly bucked and moaned and thrashed beneath them. While they took turns working her or holding her. Spanking her. Slapping her. Beating her. The violence of their interplay increased with her wantonness.

She begged them for it! She loved it!

Sam's wet palm twisted around the haft of his pistol, which he had strapped to his right hip, its weight counterbalanced by four full magazines hanging from the left side of his belt. He pondered her debauchery while measuring angles.

With a mad thought, he half-stood to charge into the house and shoot them all. He would claim that he caught two strangers molesting his neighbor under cover of the storm. Cass would be a sad case of collateral damage.

Then he thought again. He needed no excuse, since he had no intention of facing judge, jury or executioner.

Thinking this, he started for the front door. Then he stopped again. Moving as silently as he could manage, he returned to one of the home's front windows, where a loose set of curtains let warm, yellow light spill outward into the storming nightscape. Crouching there, he watched.

Just a while longer, he promised himself. *What could it hurt?*

Though her age had finally begun to show around the corners of her eyes, Cass appeared to him as beautiful as ever. *Not an ounce of fat on her hot little body*, he silently mused, *and she's still a freaky little sex machine!*

Sam pinched himself obscenely. He settled more comfortably, straightening his knees and ankles for an extended stay. His pulse and respiration hastened and deepened. A rasping tongue licked perspiring lips.

Lightning blazed the darkness at his back, flashing the windswept holler lurid white-on-blue, everything thrashing and swaying, the entire world in motion. A violent torrent without, he mused, and a rancid tempest within. Stroke for stroke, one contest paced the other.

Sam's heart raced painfully, for he felt the hand of god moving through the moment, certain and sure. Doom should fall to a flash of fulmination and a peal of thunder. His right hand shifted from his crotch to the grip of his pistol, itself a progenitor of both brilliance and percussion. Nobody would hear or see evidence of his assault – not even the men he would soon murder over her.

She would watch them die. Feel the hot spurt of their gushing blood. Ecstasy would yield to horror. Then terror. Because she would next see her old lover, Sam Dell, looming large through the threshold of her smashed doorway.

Segment 18

He imagined watching her extract herself from beneath a heap of twitching corpses, screaming his name. Begging for mercy.

"What mercy have you ever shown me?"

Sam vowed to offer her none in return. Rather, he would only ask a single question. *Why?*

"I did everything you asked me to do. More." Though he loathed the weak, whiny edge to his voice, Sam no longer cared for himself, since her most recent and most brazen sexual performance had stripped away the last tatter of his self-respect. "Why them? Why both of them, at the same time?"

If she would do all *that*, why had she refused her old lover for so long? Clearly, she had not suffered from moral impediment, while the fires of lust continued to burn brightly within her belly.

"All those years, and not one taste," he softly moaned, starting from the next flash-and-rumble, all his senses and instincts quickened by the evening's storms. "Not one touch. Not one kiss."

So much time had passed. All of it, wasted.

Watching the violent display transpire before him, Sam thought perhaps he had not been assertive enough. He wondered if he should have simply taken what he wanted. Perhaps his asking and awaiting permission had, of itself, put her off.

Supine beneath him, Belmar held Cass pressed firmly into the depths of her sofa, his corded hands gripped around her upper shoulders so his thumbs hinted at a mean strangle. Sitting on the armrest over her head, himself dangling, the kid slapped her face repeatedly using his manhood as a weapon. Sam could hear and all but feel the impact of that massive tool, so the smacks of it competed with thunder for dominance within his hearing.

Segment 18

"All this time," he gasped, "is that what she wanted?"

His stomach flared acidly, and a sinking feeling drained through his bowels. Sam rocked backward in his crouch, his face pale and his mouth hanging as wide and empty as his gaze.

Rolling his eyes skyward, he cast his lost vision into the deep black shadows of her porch awning, there looking without seeing. Instead, a mental image filled his sight, this of a demonic figure descending from darkness, death's stealthy harbinger. Black eyes. Gaping mouth. Sinister intent.

Unholy Eve, mooning through god's sacred garden. In pursuit of forbidden knowledge and carnal sin. Tempted to transgression by the sleek, scaly form of Arch Angel Samael.

While most believed the devil to present itself as a serpent from the start, Sam Dell knew his scripture better. Originally, before the fall, Samael walked on two legs and he comported himself about the garden with two arms. On casting his fallen devotee out of paradise with sinful Adam and his treacherous wife, god had stripped the serpent of its limbs, forevermore cursing the beast to traverse his forsaken wilderness on its belly. Crawling.

With the next stroke of lightning, head yet uplifted, Sam saw his namesake coiled in the awning's rafter-bound shade. Its marble eyes sparkled brightly in the after-flash while its deaf ears remained immune to thunderous assault. Wicked crimson, its forked tongue slowly protruded through the gap in its cleft lips so prone to lies. Fully extended, that flag of prurient interest flicked up and down once. Twice. Thrice. Then, as slowly as extruded, that glistening pink ribbon withdrew, and Sam knew the devil –

Segment 18

the real, actual devil – had taken his measure, no doubt having found its subject much wanting and vastly lacking.

A repetitive series of feminine screams shrieked through the walls to chase thunder into his ears. Sam need not look to know her two lovers had pounded Cass to orgasm. One of many, he suspected.

Unseen for the night, his neck burned to flush bright red. He felt his ears glowing ember-hot to suppress a high-pressure rage that welled up from the depths of his wounded being. His grip twisted tightly about the haft of his weapon, even as his engorged manhood surrendered interest in her perversity, so its frustrated throb deflated sadly. Miserably. Hopelessly.

*Why them? And, if them, why not **me**?*

Another web of sheet lightning erupted above Cassie's homestead holler. Its afterglow revealed Samael drooping more loosely from awning rafters. Its massive body sagged gracefully from one horizontal support to another, so its bulk filled the shelter of the roof from one edge of its front porch to its mate.

The devil's massive head dangled lower, moment by moment, though Sam could not detect movement to propel this motion. Silent and patient as death, the monster loomed larger and larger in his uplifted vision.

A sign from god or the devil, he thought. His short destiny descending. A prayer seemed necessary, but he could not conjure the proper words, having long ago forgotten them. Nor could he decide which deity should receive his devotion.

God had never served him well. Rather, evil had tended his interests since childhood.

Sam rarely chose the right thing. The good thing.

Setting his jaw grimly and lowering his gaze to make a final survey of the home's interior, he vowed tonight would provide no exception. Unsnapping his holster, he drew his handgun as he stood.

He turned to approach her front door, which leaned directly beneath Samael's bad counsel, so the demon worm seemed to invite and encourage his malign intent. Alternately concealed and revealed by the weather, those impenetrable black eyes monitored the man's approach without blinking or flinching. Offering no judgment. Proffering no demurs.

Pink and awesome, its mouth gaped. The storm muffled its hiss beneath an acoustic shroud of incessant, voluminous rainfall.

In the moment before Sam lifted his sodden right boot to breech his lover's door, he noticed slivers of lamplight shining all around its shattered circumference. Dimly, he recognized the handiwork of another heavy boot, so he next dully understood how Belmar and the kid had beaten him to the night's fun.

Glowering angrily, a blinding rage fell across his eyes as sometimes happened when excessive drink and emotion engulfed his thoughts. He would never properly remember the terminal events that followed. Such merciful tricks the human brain plays while suffering.

By the time he realized what had happened, Sam could already feel the mental buzz and tingle of pending unconsciousness. Starting from its edges, his vision dimmed and narrowed. Then his eyes filled with a bright white light, so he guessed this must be the mortal color of crushing. Of suffocating. Of dying.

Locked in a terrible embrace, man and serpent thrashed violently about the porch, disturbing the various plants and sparse furnishing abandoned there. Half-rotted floorboards hollowly returned sounds of their struggle like drums amplifying its desperate effects. Ultimately, this din overwhelmed the storm's monstrous tantrums to disturb the three lovers' impassioned attention.

Belmar pulled the ruined door wide, its unbalanced rotation grating across the parlor's scuffed wooden floor. Naked and panting, he stood in silhouette within a rectangle of lamplight, while his wild, crazed gaze searched the nightscape for threat.

Cat Lady's low-lying property puddled with rainwater. Countless serpents alternately coiled or glided, writhing through its pattering causeways.

Blinking to clear his vision, the wildlife agent struggled to make sense of this strange tableau as revealed intermittently by lightning bolts and the dull glow of electric lamps. Leaning forward to push the screen open a foot or so, he confirmed his original impression, verifying a ubiquitous presence of frenetic reptiles teeming all around the house, an unexpected scene given the cold deluge.

Normally, the animals would stay deep to take advantage of warm sub-surface currents during a storm. Then, too, he marked the uniform size of the swarm's individual members, each being perhaps two feet long. As he lingered, one specimen swirled across the porch before his naked toes, so Belmar could clearly identify the bloody, mucous-bound remnants of afterbirth.

"Shit," he growled, stepping backward to lock the screen. *She must have given birth directly under the house!*

When Bob Two called for a report, Belmar's shoulders bunched to remember his stiffened priority. Deciding the situation could wait until daylight and better weather, he returned to the door to its frame, subtly taking care to wedge it more firmly into place.

Then he eagerly rejoined the fun, reporting storm-related mischief and nothing more. Lighting flashed through rain-beaded windows. Thunder followed.

Segment 18

Outside, having tumbled into the home's riotous boxwood hedge, the demon worm squirmed violently against her prey while relishing newfound freedom of movement provided by the purge of birth. Once she cast her offspring into the wilderness, her duty done, she must next feast or perish. Nature allowed small forgiveness of its harsh demands.

Frustrated and starving, the serpent struggled with its prey, its powerful coils flexing against Sam's final breath to stifle his screams and his life, too. His empty hands fumbled for the handgun he had lost atop the porch, so he must claw at the serpent's hideous coils with broken fingernails. Surrounding their silent struggle, a hundred confused yet exuberant younglings swam, all skittering furiously around her like embers cast from a fire.

Segment 18

SEGMENT 19

"God damn it." Disgusted, Belmar spat into the overgrown hedge that surrounded Cat Lady's porch. Leaning against its warped and peeling rail, he measured the flood's unknown depth against his truck's known dimensions. Since it stood to its door latches in the swamp's chocolate waters, he knew four feet of sluggish runoff surrounded the house. *She might have warned me!*

Given its steady rate of flow, he expected a full day to pass before the roads cleared. Provided the storm had emptied itself of rain. Then they would walk to Bailey's store, he and Bob Two.

Cat Lady could go hang. "Bitch." Again, he spat.

Marking contrast to the state of his own pickup, Cassie's ancient piece of shit sat high and dry. She had perched it atop the last available patch of hummock not occupied by her homestead's footprint, which otherwise emerged like a tiny island at the center of its waterlogged holler.

Marking the footfalls of Bob's approach, without turning he growled, "I still owe three years' payments."

Bob somberly returned, "I think we have bigger problems."

When the kid fell silent to require Belmar's attention, the older man spun angrily. To his surprise, he confronted an armed protégé, discovering a pistol in the other's right grip.

"I found this over there," Bob tipped his head to the northern corner of Cat Lady's wraparound porch, "with this and these." He held forth a black leather billfold, its corners rounded by ages of wear, accompanied by a keyring that dangled from his fingers. "The wallet is his. The rest, too. Probably."

Smearing a haggard face with massaging fingers of one hand, Belmar absently scratched his shirtless belly with the other. Wearing only a pair of loosely belted trousers, he accepted the wallet from Bob Two, who stood fully dressed save for socks and shoes. Though wrinkled, he had laundered the khaki shirt and shorts of his uniform despite the prospects of another damp, muddy day.

Impatient and grumpy, Belmar barked, "His, who?"

Opening the billfold, he identified a familiar face. Though he appeared to be ten years younger in the photo, Sam Dell stared back at Belmar from his expired Florida driver's license.

"Shit and shit again."

For the first time, Bob Two noticed the rest of their predicament. Darting to the rail, his hands slapped empty pockets to betray frantic thoughts.

"Our gear!" he gushed miserably. "My phone! I left it locked in the glove compartment!"

"Yeah. Mine, too."

"Maybe it's all still dry," burst the kid, starting for the porch stairs. One foot poised over the murky waters, he caught himself, eyes bulging.

"Be my guest," gloomed Belmar. "They're cute little beggars – and no threat to a big boy like you – but...."

"Momma," guessed Bob Two, returning his right foot to the porch's top step. Ponderously, he climbed back to the deck, moving to place himself behind the hedge-smothered rail as though its meager shelter could protect him. Scores of diminutive serpents surrounded the property. "It is her. Isn't it?"

Though he sensed his friend wanted to hear 'no', Belmar nodded. "Oh, yeah. It's her."

"The big mother."

"The big mother," confirmed Belmar, his voice borne upon a muffled sigh. When one of her inexperienced offspring slithered across his toes, he kicked the animal off the porch and into the soup, adding, "And now a hundred little ones, each one as deadly as momma."

His ragged tone edging toward panic, Bob backed toward the little home's unhinged door. "What should we do?"

Belmar shrugged. "We pucker tight and think clearly. That's what we do."

"And then?"

"Why are you worried, Bob?" he returned stoically. Calmly. Coolly. "We've snatched a hundred snakes like this one. No sweat."

He could hear the kid shaking his head. "Uh-uh. Not a fully grown porker. Not one like *her*."

Now the older man rotated his deadliest and most earnest gaze toward his young intern. For a stern moment, he simply stared, drilling his confidence directly into Bob's head.

Then he said, "Don't forget yourself, boy. We are armed human beings. She's a dumb animal."

"A really *huge* dumb animal," Bob Two insisted stiffly, adding, "one that killed the old man. Roberto, too, probably."

"You don't know that!"

"You don't know otherwise!"

"If she ate one of them," he started hotly, before he sucked a deep, soothing breath to continue more gently, "she wouldn't be mobile enough to catch the second one. So...." Suddenly, his intended sentiment took a twisted turn.

"I guess that makes me feel better, the probability that she only ate one of the two!" Another disturbing thought obviously crossed Bob's mind. His face pinched. Exhibiting the recovered handgun, he announced, "And *we* are not armed human beings. I'm armed. You're shit out of luck."

Belmar's eyes popped. His right hand slapped his right hip. No belt. No holster. No handgun.

Next, his head snapped hard left to precede a single anxious step taken in the direction of his submerged pickup. He had locked their firearms inside the truck's toolbox, as per regs.

"Three times, shit!"

Both men jumped when she spoke from behind the screen door, her appearance unannounced. "Why are you two fools still here? Get the hell out!"

"Can we borrow your boat?"

"I don't have a boat!"

"Then we can't leave."

They could almost hear her crazy rage building before she screeched, "Then you had better start wading faster than I can fetch my shotgun!"

Neither man assumed this to be an idle threat. Belmar bolted after her, emerging moments later amid riotous, screaming protests, her only firearm in hand. He racked its slide to chamber a round, safing its action afterward.

"I feel a bit better now."

"Yeah?" groused Bob Two. "You feel better about what?"

"I feel better about watching you wade out to the truck to fetch our gear."

Eyes wide and face pale, Bob's head snapped back and forth between the two. Truck. Boss. Truck. Boss. At some point during the exchange, their demon worm slithered into his ideations. "Screw you! I quit!"

That slapped Belmar's face. He replied before he completely considered his response. "You can't quit, since I'm using the emergency powers of a duly appointed game warden to deputize you, thereby commandeering your voluntary service. For the duration!" He wondered if he actually possessed such powers, then he wondered if Bob knew better, either way.

Taking his turn to register a verbal slap, Bob Two mentally stumbled only to recover, swell and reply, "It's not 'volunteered service' if it's commandeered, dumbass!"

"You'll do as you're told, boy!"

"Or what?"

Stalemate. Each faced the other defiantly.

Eventually, returning to linger behind the mask of her screen door, Cass answered, "If you want, I could get a butcher knife and then stab you both. Problem solved."

"We don't have a problem," growled Belmar.

"Maybe, but my way would raise the nation's IQ a point or two!" After they stubbornly pressed the silence, she rejoined, "Well? Should I fetch a blade, morons?"

Both men slowly rotated their attention to their ungracious host. Bob drawled, "Lady, you're mean!"

She farted. Maybe with her mouth. Maybe for real.

"To hell with both you clowns." They heard her stomp away across her parlor's hollow floorboards. "I'm making toast. Just for me, myself. Y'all can eat shit!"

Segment 19

Rolling their eyes together, both combatants softened to meet in the middle-ground of Cat Lady's ramshackle porch. Also together, they returned to the front porch rail, where they leaned casual elbows, as good southern men will do when confronting a 'serious situation'.

Once his pulse slowed a bit, Belmar announced, "We can't shack-up with crazy-bitch for long, or somebody's going to get hurt. Obviously, one of us has to fetch our gear so we can safely wade out of here."

Bob brokered a thoughtful pause. Then he nodded.

"Right," confirmed boss. He also brokered a cogitative pause before he concluded by asking, "Can you shoot, son?"

Bob Two initially stiffened. Then his shoulders slumped. Humbly, rolling his hands to make a surly offer of it, Bob passed the pistol, answering, "Not accurately, but I could shoot you, probably by accident."

"By accident, you say?"

"Probably." Though he struggled to manage a sober expression, he could not long repress the stupid grin that quickly erupted there. "Definitely."

Belmar accepted the pistol with a shrug and a sly smile. "I guess that's better than getting shot on purpose."

"Yeah. So, maybe you should watch while I go for the gear."

Comparing pistol to shotgun, Belmar tipped a cavalier head. "Okay, Bob, you talked me into it."

Pointedly leaning the latter weapon against an awning support – far away from Cat Lady's ruined front door – he next racked the pistol's action to check for a live chamber. Then he dropped its clip to verify its load, returning this to its place with a comforting mechanical snap.

Segment 19

"Are you ready to go now?" When Bob nodded, he pointedly switched the weapon's catch from 'SAFE' to 'FIRE'.

Then he led the kid to the steps. He shook himself loose around his neck and shoulders, careful to keep his weapon's muzzle pointed into the water, which lapped gently against lower stairs. Finally, he nodded.

While Bob slowly and carefully waded down the home's steps and into the tepid flood, the heavens opened again. A fine mist began to fall while a rising wind promised further deluge to come. Indeed, the sky darkened perceptibly as he felt his way through the drowned switchgrass that mottled Cassie's unkempt lawn.

Following the kid with his eyes, Belmar held the pistol at his waist, bracing it at the ready using both hands. Moment to moment, he scanned the surface of the soup, searching for telltale stirs of a large serpent. He knew the monsters could swim deep, but he also knew those flood waters ran shallow across the top of Cassie's hummock. A porker so large would likely stir the bottom muck as it passed.

Wading to his waist and then his lower chest, Bob approached the truck's locked cab without incident. When a juvenile serpent swam toward his young companion – no doubt looking for dry land rather than food – Belmar lifted his weapon, took careful aim and then POP!

Bob jumped and screamed, cursing. Belmar shrugged into the kid's glare. "Practice."

Huffing and blowing angrily, Bob returned to his task. He pulled the driver's side door latch, finding it locked. Groaning, he rolled his eyes.

Turning to confront Belmar about the obvious oversight, he saw the man stretching forward in mid-toss. Sparkling and tinkling metallically, the required keyring

Segment 19

tumbled across overcast skies, landing at his knees with a splash and a PLOP.

"Nice catch, kid!"

"Asshole."

Bob felt along the muddy, weedy bottom with anxious feet. He struggled to parse the sensation of roots from grass stalks from the cluster of keys.

After making several attempts to retrieve them with his toes, he scanned the water's surface for danger. Between stretches of dancing foliage and dim shadows drawn by a hidden sun, dappling raindrops cast endless circular ripples over all. Nothing large and hungry seemed to be swimming forward, ready to devour him.

Stooping lower and lower, he fumbled through the muck with nervous fingers. The improved sensory resolution of these appendages better informed his quest, but the missing keys still eluded him. He began to think they had somehow drifted on the sluggish current, though his better intuition discouraged such impossible thoughts. *They sank straight to the bottom where they fell.* Bending his knees so he could thrust his hands deeper into the detritus, his nose hovered just above the flood.

This lowered perspective severely limited his field of view. Accordingly, his pulse increased with a brooding surge of anxiety.

"I think they landed a bit further to the right," shouted Belmar, motioning with his free hand. "Your other right, kid!"

Mumbling beneath his breath, he shifted this way and then that. Something cold and smooth and hard slid between his left thumb and forefinger.

Instantly, his spine straightened rigidly, bursting his upper body and limbs from the soup amid a whitewater jolt.

Segment 19

In this shocked pose, he froze, eyes bulging, all color drained from his face.

Perhaps hours – more likely seconds – later, his senses snapped into focus and he heard Belmar calling his name, demanding to know what had happened. What had he seen? What had he felt? Was it her?

Bob nodded stiffly. Belmar leaned backward; eyes wide. He shook his head and told Bob that he must be mistaken.

"She's long gone, since giving birth," he calmed the kid. "They do that, you know. It's nature's way of giving the kiddies a headstart. Reduced competition. Understand?"

Appearing to doubt, Two licked trembling lips. Anyway, he remained alive and he had already come so far. Turning a full circle in the chest-deep flood, he determined to try again. No half-measures this time.

Completely submerging to a crouch on the bottom, he conducted a more thorough inch-by-inch survey of the tangled sawgrass and sedge. Moments before his lungs burst, he snagged something that tinkled musically through the gurgling liquid.

Darting sharply to the surface again, he lifted the ring high, sputtering and blowing. With his free hand, he plowed muck from eyes, nostrils, ears and mouth, gasping for air.

Ignoring boss's shouts of encouragement, being better motivated by concerns for his own life, Belmar quickly fitted the most obvious candidate key into the truck's door lock. It popped and the hatch opened with a soggy clunk of its mechanism.

Murky water surged into and then out of the truck's cabin. Bits of paper and plastic swirled away atop the Everglades' all but imperceptible current.

Segment 19

His guts rolled the same way when he confirmed the ruin of their electronics. Hoping dry rice could help, he retrieved the devices and their chargers, stuffing these into the breast pockets of his shirt.

Returning to the vehicle's exterior, he unlocked its toolbox to extract their webbing, gear and riot guns. As an afterthought prompted by Belmar's insults, he also retrieved the man's pistol, belt, holster and spare mags.

He confirmed completion of his mission. "Is that all you want? You're sure? Absolutely positive?"

Slamming the toolbox lid too hard, Bob Two paused to gather all the straps and bands and packs that he had gathered around his shoulders. Satisfied of his load's security, he turned to wade back to Cat Lady's porch.

Raindrops made Lilypad circles atop the deluge. Wind-driven foliage danced wildly before a rising gale that promised yet more rainfall. Overhead, the heavens darkened. Renewed strokes of lightning beget increasingly savage peals of thunder.

"Great," he groaned miserably, holding his arms high while waddling toward safety, "more r-."

Then he simply disappeared with a vicious downward jerk of his body. One moment there. Gone the next.

Belmar shook his head to clear his vision. He stepped forward to descend the porch's top step as though this meager reduction of distance might improve his understanding. A lurid strobe of fulmination momentarily blinded him. Resultant thunder deafened.

Rain fell. The dappled surface swirled gently.

No thrashing signs of struggle broke the surface. Bob Two apparently made no attempt to fight for his life. Only a vague momentum in the resultant wake hinted at the monster's escape.

It had dragged the boy directly under the truck. Though it might be a result of wave action, he thought he detected a subtle but violent roll of the vehicle's shocks and springs.

To improve his perspective of the truck's far side, he moved to the farthest corner of Cat Lady's porch. As he had suspected, a definite trail of roiling silt marked the worm's egress. She had immediately dragged the boy into deeper water, no doubt coiling and crushing his body as she withdrew.

Impotent and helpless, Belmar stood at the warped and splintered railing. Rainfall and lightning shadows made a mockery of his supervision since he never saw the boy again. Not one broaching gasp for air. No upward thrusting grasps for aid. Nothing.

Behind him, his thunder-ravaged ears detected a rising sound of human merriment. Standing behind the rusted mask of her screen door, Cass had watched the entire episode. Its foreseeable outcome amused her, so she cackled madly to see Belmar's stunned reaction when he turned to confront her, enraged.

Scarcely able to speak for laughing, she gushed, "You look like a mouthful of warm pudding just turned to cold shit."

His face burning bright red, Belmar spun on his heel to hide his shame and make a final search for the boy. *What should I tell his mother? Certainly not the whole truth!*

Another troubling thought chased the thunder. Shaking a marveling head, he hissed, "The bitch swam away with all our gear, too."

SEGMENT 20

"Fourteen rounds left in the pistol," he quietly announced, "and you have half-a-box of birdshot for the scattergun. So, ten rounds. Of twenty-gauge – a woman's load."

Sitting across her scuffed and use-worn kitchen table, Cass dismissed his stupidity by sucking on her teeth in an audibly dissatisfied way. "As you likely noticed, I *am* a woman."

"As is our demon worm."

Her delicately veined fingers fumbled with a familiar box. Its label told him how much "Healthy Cats Love Them!"

"They're all gone by now," she mused, her tone distracted and thoughtful, though oddly lacking in regret and sorrow. "Every one of them."

"After all that's happened, you're worrying about a pack of mangy strays?"

Eyes flashing violently, the shadow of her inner demon crossed Cat Lady's twisted countenance. She spat, "I don't care about the cats, fool, except their obvious absence makes our problem a simple one."

Corrected, Belmar accepted the cruelty of her remarks as being well-deserved. For now.

To be clear, he replied, "Because we're it now. The only sizeable items left on her menu."

Pontificating her following remarks, blue-white lighting flashed the interior of her home, the sun having hidden behind storm clouds, which rolled miles deep overhead. Thunder chased through after-image shadows to trouble their eyes and ears, both.

She said, "With so much rain, we're three days away from dry roads. At least."

Unhappily disturbed, Belmar's jaw dropped. Before he could stop himself, he whined – as though speaking to his recalcitrant mother, "Three days? You're sure?"

"Maybe five." She shrugged. "Depends."

Disgusted, she smashed the box in her fists and then she spun in her rickety chair to toss the refuse into her kitchen trashcan. Belmar wondered if she always wore so little around the house, or if she had especially dressed that way to seduce him.

Then again, he realized she had no need to seduce, since he stiffened on a cool breeze while in her company. Strangely, when he attempted to decipher his attraction to her, his understanding only penetrated so far into the tangled fibers of a perverse and extremely sexualized psyche. Few practical answers seemed apparent.

Perhaps cued by his gaze, Cass gathered the loose lapels of her sheer robe, pulling them into overlap across her flat tummy. No need to worry for the tits, her scarcely-endowed mother had often remarked, since she didn't have more than a rudimentary pair of bug bites.

Nipples, though, she possessed in wonderful abundance. No hiding those. His eyes fixated on them. She watched him lick pouting lips.

Tossing disgusted hands, she rose to make tea. She knew his gaze would follow her hips as though she had tied strings to them, but Cass had long ago surrendered the struggle against male horniness.

By welcoming a ripe set of testicles into her kitchen, she had invited him between her legs, too. At least, this is how men like Belmar understood such an arrangement.

To assume dominant control of her household, he only needed to pin her down with a savage grip applied to her throat. That, and steal her shotgun, of course.

Her back turned, she dared to lick her own wanton lips, tasting him there. In her mouth. Atop her tongue. Him and the boy.

No dark thoughts of Bob's fate crossed her mind to worry her heart. Like all human props in her play, he had made his entrance, portrayed his part and then he had exited stage left. Good riddance.

"She couldn't swallow him whole," spoke Cass, pondering a stark and ugly truth behind eyes wide open. "I've seen it before when they're starving. They work at it for hours, only to retch everything up again in surrender, hungrier than ever."

Propping Sam's pistol atop her small kitchen table, Belmar busied himself with an oily rag. Polishing the steel, he attempted to avoid unpleasant thoughts, but Cass would not allow him such comfort.

"Their eyes get bigger than their stomachs," she continued, popping the pilot of her stove to start a propane burner beneath her kettle. Next, she tinkled cups and spoons, generously preparing a serving for her unpleasant guest, though he had not asked. "But I suppose they must get the measure of themselves, one way or another."

Watching the slash-and-burn sashay of her hips as predicted, Belmar grimaced. Like her, he scarcely felt a thing for the passing of the Bobs, and he believed he would largely escape recrimination for their loss given circumstances. Albeit, at the cost of his job. Maybe. Her mocking tone bothered him though, since the ridicule of any woman jabbed at the heart of his most intimate and personal weaknesses.

She probably knew the male mind well enough to anticipate this shortcoming. Anticipate and exploit it.

Since the old lady had started working him first, Belmar flatly returned, "I guess you don't need me any longer, since you finally managed to kill your old beau after all."

Scoffing with a soft, wet noise formed atop her tongue, Cass immediately returned, "Maybe. Maybe not. If anyone killed him, I would jot that failure on your side of the ledger, Agent Wonder-Boy. Or aren't you the mighty white hunter?"

He ground his teeth. He polished Sam's handgun. He eyeballed the gyro of her waist. The jut of her tanned, athletic legs. Her perfect feet and hands. That vicious gray head.

Pointedly, he asked, "Why do you think he dropped his wallet and pistol on your front porch last night, of all nights?"

"I told you before, the man is-."

"*Was.*"

"-a pervert. A rapist. Just like you."

Now Belmar grinned lecherously. "Oh, I get it. He stopped slapping you around, and then he was no fun any longer."

Oblivious to his implications, she tipped her head. Pouring hot water into a pair of unmatched cups, she told him, "Something like that, I guess. You've been balling me for weeks. You can probably guess my hang-ups."

"Yeah," he gushed, this word exploding unbidden from his lungs so he must hastily follow with the truth, despite his better desires, "and you certainly know mine."

"Kid, I knew what you are before you ever climbed my porch steps." She turned from her labors bearing two steaming brews backed by two very pointed nipples. Long, luxurious and thick, they popped the gauzy material of her robe, more than compensating for the diminutive stature of her breasts.

"My face is up here, champ," she quipped, sliding into her chair as she pushed a cup across the table to interrupt his nervous gunplay. "Don't you ever get tired?"

"What do you think?"

"Anyway, we have no time for that. You need to get the hell out of here and I need to get to work."

"Doing what?"

"That's none of your god-damned business." She blew her tea. She mocked him with her sparkling green eyes. Ultimately, she quipped, "You really are some kind of punk. Do you even know what kind?"

Though he had no fondness for hot tea, Belmar warmed his palms on the cracked mug. His countenance pale and sober, clearly worried for himself – mostly his truck – the man lifted one shoulder in an uncertain half-shrug.

"I know I screwed up," he admitted, speaking slowly and deliberately, "and I also know I don't want to suffer for it. Anyway, I don't think I should. Do you?"

"I think I don't give a shit either way." She sipped delicately, wincing to retract too eager lips. "Same as I know better than tangle with the law. I already know how that game ends, and I won't go through it all again. Not for anybody, but especially not for a useless man."

Segment 20

"I'm not useless!" he spat too vehemently, so he instantly regretted the crack in his demeanor. She knew exactly where to strike!

He chewed his lip. He tried again.

"What can you tell them, anyway?" Again, too petulantly. He pouted. "I didn't do anything wrong."

She sipped successfully this time. "You didn't do anything right, either."

"Why are you such a bitch?"

"Why are you such a dick?"

He marveled slackly. "You are hot and cold, lady! Will you *please* tell me what I did to piss you off this time?"

Fixing a hateful mask onto her face, she spat back, "Uh, let's see. You kicked in my front door. You assaulted and kidnapped me at gunpoint in my own living room. You gang-raped me with your pal. You-."

"Now hold on just a god damned minute there, you crazy bitch! You've made that claim once too often, and it stopped being funny the first time! Nobody raped anybody!"

"Explain the door! Explain the bruises! Explain the semen that you blasted all over my furniture!"

Once more, Belmar's eyes bulged impossibly. He thought his head should explode from the pressure, and he could not possibly understand how the morning had taken such a bizarre and deadly turn! His mouth opened and closed impotently since he momentarily forgot all the rules of English syntax.

What could a man say to such accusations? What *should* he say?

When she leapt to her feet, he thought she had decided to attack him or run for her life, having clearly provoked him beyond all hope of sane recovery. Like her front door, he stood to confront her, butt-sprung and warped far beyond reason, shattered in his frame. The pistol hung from his right fist, as forgotten as his capacity to comprehend human language.

He expected a fight-or-flight response from his provocative host. Instead, she turned to fetch a rag from one of her kitchen drawers. Not a knife. Not a gun.

Then she came to him as he stood beside the table, stiffly seizing with rage. Taking his hand, she tended a deep and heavily bleeding wound, where his shattered mug had cut through the webbing between his right thumb and forefinger.

Incredulous and speechless with anger, he dully watched her wrap his injury, never mind the spilled tea that steamed atop her table. Regardless of shattered pottery shards that threatened bare feet atop her kitchen floor.

Submissive and expectant, she dropped his injured extremity to stand demurely before him. Her gaze rose to his chin. No farther.

Stepping backward and away from her, Belmar measured her puzzling intent with a wild, savage gaze. Heartbeats later, he slapped her viciously across her face, seized her lithe body in powerfully corded arms, and then dragged her to her bedroom, screaming.

Segment 20

SEGMENT 21

"Did you really kill your husband?" asked Belmar, his voice soft and low like the falling light of evening, his tone void of judgment and only vaguely curious.

They lay in her bed, twisted in her sheets, her blankets tossed to the floor. A ceiling fan spun lazily overhead to draft perspiring flesh that quivered with spent sexual ecstasy.

Cass rolled away from him, but she remained in the tuck of his left arm, her head laying in the crook of his elbow. Dreamily, she nuzzled her hair out of her face.

She asked, "Is that what Sam told you?"

"Yeah."

"That's what he tells everybody when he isn't telling some other lie. Only you can decide what you believe, Belmar."

Her use of his name caught the man's attention. His head turned to breathe through her hair. Strangely, he had never felt happier or more content. *Crazy bitch.*

"I still haven't heard your side of the story."

"Would it matter?"

Since her tone seemed genuine, Belmar took time to ponder her question with all due sincerity. Then he nodded, returning his face to the free air of her bedroom, where he watched the fan's spiral shadows stir its walls and eaves to pace his torpid heartbeat. "Yeah, Cass. I think it matters."

Sighing leadenly, she tried to recall the last time she had even attempted to tell anyone the truth. After so many years, the lie seemed better, if only because its details at least justified the banishment and isolation she had suffered since. The truth rendered everything harder, more painful and more difficult to accept.

Cassandra Lee Winchell, outsider and damned northern Yankee, made an easy target. Everyone took potshots at every possible opportunity.

Yet Crazy Cat Lady kept the strangers at bay. Her unpredictable nature and vicious reputation answered all queries unasked since everyone already knew her to be a wicked killer. A crazy bitch who traveled everywhere with a pistol in her poke and Florida's self-defense laws fresh in her mind. A wanton woman who would conspire with her paramour to murder her husband in his own parlor.

"I suppose Sam told you we were lovers, too," she guessed absently. When Belmar nodded, she added, "Another lie."

"Right," he concurred, "I can see that now."

"You can?"

"Yeah, baby. I can."

For a moment she stiffened, and he thought she might bolt, probably for her shotgun. Then she relaxed more deeply into his embrace, which he folded protectively around her.

Her voice a grateful whisper, she accepted his devotion by offering her own. "Okay, I believe you."

Lightning. Thunder. Rainfall once more pattered her moss-grown rooftiles.

Segment 21

Cass shivered. With his free hand, Belmar drew the crumpled sheet higher across their waists despite the holler's oppressively humid cloister.

Confessing, she said, "Lonnie loved Sam Dell, but I never liked the man. I never trusted him. Everything he touched turned to shit. Everything he ever said turned out to be a lie."

"Even the football-hero stories?"

He felt her head move against his bicep, nodding. "Especially that. Oh, he scored a few touchdowns during high school, this much is true, but he never won a scholarship to Florida State. He never ran a single yard in college."

Confused, Belmar recalled his one and only visit to the man's untidy home. Again and again, their conversation had invariably returned to the game and all the memorabilia that Sam had pinned to his walls.

"I saw the press clippings. The awards."

Cass groaned to hear this tired protest again. "Somehow, Sam heard about another player with the same name, who coincidentally started at FSU during what would have been his freshman year. True enough, he moved away from home for a while to prosper the lie – nobody knows where he really went. The next summer, he came back, of course, and nothing to show for his troubles."

Her body bucked with a soft chuckle. "Strangely enough, Sam Dell – the *real* player, I mean – continued to rack impressive collage stats until he graduated. Three years after *our* Sam Dell came back home to live with mom and dad."

Belmar chewed his lower lip, contemplating the strange lies that people tell. Chiefly, he wondered why they should bother.

Segment 21

As though answering his unspoken questions, Cass added, "That was Sam, though. He would tell a lie to his hangman. After so many tall tales, I quickly decided the man was insane. He knew I could see right through him, too, and he hated me for it."

"Hated you? When I spoke to him, he seemed to dote on you from afar like a whipped puppy."

"You saw lust, nothing more. Oh, he always wanted me, but only because I was Lon's girl. Something he could never have. Not because Lon wouldn't share me with him – we often invited couples and singles into our bed."

"He wanted you because you're a beautiful person, inside and out." Rolling left, he pulled her into the spoon-shaped fold of his body, intertwining his legs with hers.

"You really believe that," she marveled.

"It's true."

Passing once more through a resistant moment, Cass eventually accepted his embrace. Her body eased into his like something warm and pliable poured into a mold.

"I suppose that made things worse. They fought about it, from time to time. Usually after Sam heard about one of our dalliances."

"Of course, you never dropped such hints in his presence."

He couldn't see her mischievous grin. "I was jealous, I suppose, and it was a game. At first."

"Then?"

Another leaden sigh. A deeper snuggle. She shivered.

"Then, I finally understood the danger."

Belmar allowed the thoughtful pause that followed. He sensed the strain of a psychological dam bulging to burst, and he knew she required such release.

Segment 21

She continued, saying, "Sam is – was – insane. Truly psychopathic. They're a strange lot, that kind. He could be so charming, but so obviously fake at the same time. Everyone could easily see through the fool's thin veneers."

"Everyone, except your husband."

Another nod. "His best friend," she stated these words in a way that suggested sarcasm and 'air quotes'. "Watching them together, I eventually realized what was happening. The rest of us – Lon's true friends and family – we could see around the façade so easily because we weren't the focus of Sam's affection. His lies weren't made for us."

"It was Lon."

"Sam was obsessed. Most of us came to accept his antics as simply odd or eccentric. He was the village idiot. The town joke. To everyone but Lon Seminole, who believed just about everything that Sam Dell ever said."

She rolled onto her right side, lifting her head higher onto Belmar's shoulder to better manage the added elevation of her neck. Her soft cheek gently nuzzled the firmness of his arm.

"Even the football stuff?"

Now Cass stiffened, but she refused to relax. Her tone hardened again, she answered, "Especially the football stuff. That's what got Lon killed."

A moment of silence passed. Belmar chased possibilities.

He guessed, "When Sam returned home that summer pretending to be on hiatus from the team, something happened that tipped Lon toward the truth."

"*I* happened. In fact, push come to shove, I was probably the reason that Sam left home in the first place. Once I realized he was full of it, I started needling him the way any female might do with a rival in the room. Because I quickly came to see Sam that way, you know. As a rival for Lon's attention and affection.

"You have to remember that we were very young. Young and dumb and naïve and just so damned horny all the time. I was a seventeen-year-old runaway from Syracuse. Sam was a year older than me and Lonnie a year older than he when we all first met. Lon and I married two months after he picked me up on the side of a highway just north of here. That spring, my husband graduated high school and only weeks later his mother died in a terrible accident, leaving us this place and that truck parked in my yard.

"The following summer, Sam somehow managed to graduate, too – not that it's a huge academic leap given the standards of local schools – and this after he boasted about all the agents and scouts that had been following him around town, pestering him to sign at this or that university, and offering him uncommon sums of money. Naturally, nobody but Sam ever saw or heard a thing about it all."

"But you knew better."

"I started to wonder about that clown from the moment we first met. Syracuse overflows with that type. Townies that compete with rich frat boys for the temporary affection of their best girls. Too many of them grease their dates' panties with exaggerations and lies. For some, this becomes a habit and then, eventually, a way of life. Sam was that kind, I never understood why."

"Yeah, this is no place to brag."

"Everybody knows everything about everybody else, and nobody has something their neighbor doesn't. With few exceptions, of course, but the Dell family was never an exception of any kind. They've been redneck peckerwoods since the dawn of time, I suppose, and none of them any good. To themselves or anyone else."

"This is not so for the Seminole family?"

"Lonnie's family was a blend of locals and natives. Family legend says one of the last aboriginal uprisings left his great-grandfather orphaned as an infant, making him an unknown ward of the state. That's how they took the name 'Seminole'. They're named after their tribal nation. Sort of."

"Sort of?"

"It's an unnecessarily long and complicated story, really, most of it sourced in ignorance. The real difference that it makes around here is simple. Money. Lon's family received a sizeable lifelong stipend from the federal government, which allowed his people to live slightly better than average. That's all."

"So, in a way, Sam's relationship with your husband improved the man's status. Like that?"

"Maybe. I only knew one thing in the beginning. Lon spent too much time with his so-called best friend. I could clearly see how Sam manipulated my husband, and that peaked my claws, by itself."

Belmar grinned. "As his wife, that was *your* job."

"Exactly! Their relationship might not have much bothered me, even then, except so many of Sam's choices and behaviors were bad. Not just bad, but stupid, too. And dangerous."

"How so?"

Once more, Cass stiffened and then relaxed again, deciding she should reveal all. "Well, for one thing, he got his younger brother killed a few years before I arrived." Shuddering, perhaps having confronted this truth for the first time, herself, she conceded, "Hell, he probably murdered the boy in a fit of jealously, though that's not the

Segment 21

story he told. In his version of events, his brother drowned while recovering a fishing lure, or something of the kind. No matter which way he staged the event, though, I thought the whole scenario smacked of bullshit. Maybe this is what started it, him and me.

"Because after I heard this story for the first time, I saw Sam in a different light. From then forward, nothing he allowed seemed gospel to me, and I started watching – and listening – carefully." She paused to allow a peal of thunder pass, adding, "Funny thing though."

"You couldn't make Lon believe any of it."

"Not a word. Not at first."

Belmar widened his supposition. "Then Sam started bragging about the football scholarship."

Nodding again, she curled deeper into his cage-like embrace, his arms folded around her neck and shoulders. "I think it was his way of driving a wedge between Lon and me, and it almost worked. We had been fighting off and on through that first year of marriage, mostly about Sam's tall-tales of frat-parties and loose groupies, let the good times roll."

Her lover marveled. "How did Sam think it would end, once Lon actually arrived at campus?"

"And why did the fool ever even imagine that Lon would go away with him? You see? The man is certifiably crazy."

New and foreboding information flooded Belmar's consideration. "You mean to say that you knew he was murderously psychotic."

Cass chewed her lip. "I didn't understand the situation in those terms at the time. I was just a naïve kid. A dropout. But, yes, I eventually realized what he was, mostly based on things he said about his brother. The way

Segment 21

he acted. Like he was relieved by the boy's death. A burden removed."

"So, he went away to school in the fall, even though the scholarship was a lie?"

"Yes. He mailed press clippings and photographs and he wrote long, detailed letters to Lonnie that bragged about all the wild times. Meanwhile, he was probably living in a hostel and eating out of dumpsters. Nobody knows where he went or what he was doing while he was away, but everyone knew when he returned. That's when it happened."

Feeling an urge resultant from their last bout of sexual excess, Belmar gently tugged his arm to free himself. After he returned from her bathroom, he sat on her bed's edge to draw on his shorts and trousers, though he left his belt unbuckled.

Rolling atop their lone sheet, he reclined on his stomach beside her, facing her back since she remained rolled into a fetal curl. Pointedly, she held her silence, so he knew she required a prompt to finish her sordid history.

"He said something about a party. Your anniversary."

"What else did he say about it?"

Belmar sighed wearily. Rolling onto his back, he wondered why every human-thing must be so damned complicated.

"He said you had grown tired of Lon by then; that you two had grown apart. You were afraid of being homeless again, and you had fallen in love with Sam when he returned."

"Yeah. Sam Dell, the football hero."

"He told me you seduced him as soon as he came back. Then you visited him almost every night after your husband fell asleep, each night working him closer and closer to doing the deed. Finally, you presented an ultimatum. When he couldn't decide, you pressured him by exploiting his weaknesses. You convinced him to delay his return to spring training camp and then you talked him into canceling his future, altogether. To have you forever, he only needed to do one thing."

When Belmar took his turn to fall silent, requiring a prompt, Cass rolled from cover at last. She drew the toes of her left foot through the sparse hair of his corded chest. "And?"

"After the party, during a storm much like this one, you convinced him to do it. He arrived at the appointed hour unarmed though, having decided to confess your collective sins, take a beating, and save his best friend's life instead."

"Eve in the garden," she softly whispered, stirring his peaked nipples with her ankle, "forever tempting Adam's fall."

"Is that how it happened?"

"Everyone blamed me the same way. I suppose I deserved the blame, too, in the beginning. Before I understood who – and what – Sam Dell had become. Or always was. After, though... afterward, I was only frightened. Of him. Of what he would do, once his bubble burst. Because it was always going to burst. People like him manage things that way. They love the drama. The self-pity."

"The rage and violence."

"Yeah. That, too, in the end. In every lie, a hint of truth. Lon and I threw the party, as Sam described. It was a typical local affair. Too much to eat, too much to drink, and too many deep, dark secrets. Naively, being so damned young, I thought the truth would bind us together, us against him, the monster that seemed so determined to twist my husband's mind and poison his marriage. Sam's lies seemed too preposterous to conceive, let alone believe!

"Of course, I was an outsider then as now, but I should have anticipated the tangled lines of bullshit that bind such people together. Syracuse was no different, only colder in every way."

"Something happened at the party," he guessed.

"No, that's what surprised me. Nothing happened. Oh, a few contemporaries teased him, once I confronted him with the truth, but nobody seemed to care. Sam joked his way through the evening, and I forgot all about it for being just another Sam-Dell-related incident. Lon certainly couldn't care less, since he was already forgetting his old best friend, given my dutiful attention to his every trifling need."

"You hadn't seduced Sam, as he claims."

"He always made my skin crawl. I told you, he frightened me."

"You didn't convince him to kill your husband that night."

"That night, Lon and I tidied after the party, made love and then passed out." Cass rolled onto her elbow, propping her head with that hand, so her free fingers could spin wool atop Belmar's chest. "Just before dawn, Sam began pounding on our bedroom windows, which is how we awakened. Obviously, he was violently intoxicated. By the time Lon stepped into the living room, Sam kicked in our front door. Before they exchanged a single rational word, he immediately shot his so-called best friend directly in his heart. Lon hit the floor dead at the end of his last stride."

"Where were you?"

"Standing just behind my husband in the hallway. When he fell, it was just me and Sam and that smoking pistol hanging from his hand."

Thunder. Lightning. Torrents.

"Then what happened?"

Her tone wistful and unemotional, perhaps for having long ago reconciled the requisite pain, Cass answered, "Oh, he beat the hell out of me while he raped me for hours. He intended to kill me afterward. Probably kill himself, too.

"I knew how he wanted the three of us to end. More importantly, I knew why. Like husbands will do, Lonnie had told me his every darkest secret. Everything. Sam couldn't understand that sort of trust, so I used it against him, and I talked him out of killing me that night. The truth is just that simple."

Belmar pondered the various twists of human nature while a dismal, storm-shrouded sun faded west. One darker shade of gloom replaced another, both within his thoughts and without Cat Lady's overgrown homestead.

"The truth of how, maybe," he ultimately allowed, "but I don't think the truth of why seems as clear."

"In a way, I think it is. That night, Sam expected Lon to make a threesome with him, something that we had done many times with others, a few of them having attended the same party. Lon made the attempt, too, one of many. I'm the one who said 'no'. Sam demanded to know why, and I told him to his face. He disgusted me. When he threw a tantrum, threatening and humiliating me, Lon sent him home in a tumble. The story is as old as the serpent and the garden. So, simple, after all. Don't you agree?"

Grumbling, Belmar sucked a sour tongue. The day's unexpected events played through his thoughts.

She guessed, "You're thinking about the pistol and the wallet."

"And how the old man's house straddles your access to the main road. He intended to kill you tonight."

"He intended to kill us all. Finally, after all these years."

"Why?"

Shrugging, she curled sideways to pull the chain on a lamp, extinguishing all but the natural light of her bedroom windows. "I don't know, Belmar. Why does a psychopath do anything?"

"So, what? You lied for him about what happened?"

"I didn't need to lie because Sam got to the law first. By the time the sheriff's deputy drove all this way, the fool had already told the locals so many whoppers – and recanted each one, too – that nobody could decide what to believe."

"The village idiot."

"The town liar. Of course, I knew the truth. I told everyone the same thing I'm telling you now, word for word."

"And nobody believed you?"

"Everybody believed me, especially the law. Four decades ago, believing and proving were two totally different concepts, apparently. So, that's how they left it all these years. An open case. A rancid scandal."

"Sam Dell living at the end of your drive."

"Off and on since he returned from prison. Yeah."

Lightning flashed the darkness. Belmar jumped and felt grateful that she had not seen, then he immediately guessed she had felt the motion through her bed. Thunder quickly followed to stifle such petty worries.

"He threatened you?"

In turn, Belmar felt her shrug through the springs. "He didn't need to threaten me. Their apathy made his point. Like I said, I was an outsider then, and I'm an outsider still. Some ideas never change and, so, some small-town crimes go unpunished."

A final ugly thought nagged. "Why did you stay?"

"This is my home. Whether the locals accept me or not, I'm a Floridian woman living alone. I armed myself, and then I dared him to come back."

Ah. Belmar understood at last.

"Revenge."

"You bet your ass, kid. So long as Sam chose to live his selfish life the way he always had, I felt safe enough, since he knew my murder would inevitably come back to him. Besides, whenever he finally chose to step-off – and he always would do – I simply looked forward to blasting him in the face with my shotgun, free and clear. It was bound to happen, eventually. Turns out, last night should have been the night."

"Too bad." Belmar felt slumber's oblivion curling around his mind to dull the edge of awareness. He yawned and stretched massively. "Our demon worm spared you the trouble."

Her voice distant and fuzzy, Belmar heard her reply, "Maybe." Then he slept to suffer violent, crushing dreams.

SEGMENT 22

Cass awakened stiffly. Perhaps sourced in dimly recalled nightmares, her stomach burned frightfully. Her guts crawled.

Opening sleep-clotted eyes, she scanned early morning shadows wherever darkness poured into the corners and eaves of her sparsely furnished bedroom. Nothing seemed amiss. Nothing out of order.

Then she remembered her present situation. *No*, her stomach warned her, *this is something more*. Something worse.

Many times, that secret inner voice had spared her from mischief. Long ago, she had learned to listen, because its timely warnings had kept her alive during all those lost months spent fleeing the winter of '77.

She had learned how a pleasant smile and a cool demeanor could mask violent intent and evil thoughts. The same way a person no longer sees scaly camouflage after a serpent's first strike, she could only see the snake. Long before she met Sam Dell, Cass had grown to know such men all too well.

Several would-be highway benefactors proved to be monsters rather than men. Worse, if evil could be a religion, then her own stepfather had been a high priest of cruelty and wickedness. Of sexual deviance.

Her mother had known. Unspoken and vile though the abuse had seemed to young Cassandra Lee Winchell, her dependent and uneducated mother understood this to be the price that all women paid, having simply been born with vaginas.

Not so, her daughter. As soon as she grew old enough to know better, Cass left home in search of better options.

Too quickly, she learned to extrapolate her home life to the wider world, too, and not much changed from one day to the next. No matter which way she turned, no matter how she determined to arrive there, her existence devolved to a simple equation. Pussy for blank.

Blank might be a dry bed or a hot meal, the offer of something necessary and good. More often, blank represented an absence of something bad. She might eat or suffer a beating.

Mother taught her to accept her lot as unavoidable. Young Cassie identified two alternate choices, instead. Flight or fight.

Acceptance seemed like slow suicide. Yet even a determined teenage runaway is a still only a teenage runaway. Flight seemed easiest. At first.

Then Sam taught her a terminal truth. Since her last close contact with that animal, she invariably chose to fight.

She sat upright. That inner voice screamed.

Belmar's absence conspired with oppressive silence to recall her condition. Making a second, better informed survey of the room's interior, her eyes focused through the half-light. Outside, morning threatened, so its dull glow confirmed an absence of clouds. An inevitable stifle descended upon the 'Glades. Driven mad with motion only

Segment 22

hours earlier, now the overgrown holler simply dripped, steaming.

When her survey strayed to the far side of her bed – the side where Belmar had fallen asleep – she noted an absence of bedside bric-a-brac. Daring to cinch her way silently across her damp and rumpled mattress, she found a lamp fallen to the floor. Belmar's discarded trousers stretched there, too, as though making an empty leap for the door.

Beyond, her home's main hallway loomed darkly, ensconced in the night's fading moon shadow. Sitting straighter, Cass perked canny ears. Could she hear a slow, rhythmic sigh passing in and out through the open doorway? A low but steady hiss, perhaps?

No. The air hung heavy and still.

Curling sideways to check beside her bed, Cass slipped onto the floor to dress as quickly and quietly as she could manage, though her boots remained out of reach. In the living room. *Sam.*

Something had happened during the previous night, otherwise he would not have abandoned his belongings on her porch the way he had done. Yet, that bad man obviously remained alive, and he had clearly returned.

Perhaps Belmar rose early. Maybe he heard a noise, too, or maybe he only wanted coffee. Entering into the parlor, he had perhaps confronted her perverted stalker. She could only guess what might have happened next.

Then she reconsidered. Given recent passage of the storm, Cass suspected her young partner had gone missing much earlier in the night, while thunder and deluge masked the resultant struggle. Otherwise, even in the case of sudden death, she should have awakened to hear the drag of a heavy body through such oppressive silence.

Had Belmar and Sam sat together all night? Doing or saying what?

On cat-quiet feet, she moved across the dimly lit room to its doorway. There she lingered, ears perked. Again, she felt as much as heard the steady see-saw rasp of constricted respiration. *Shhh-shhh. Shhh-shhh.* Back and forth. In and out. Softly, a contented snore perhaps.

Walking on the balls of her feet, she eased through the threshold and along the corridor. She paused at each niche or doorway, listening.

That odd sound emanated from her parlor. With each step taken in that direction, the detail and nuance of its register improved within her hearing.

Soon, she confirmed the nature of this strange sound, since she clearly heard an unmistakable cycle of respiration. Glancing backward, she thought she should return to her bedroom to escape through its windows.

Except, that little voice warned her. No.

She moved forward again. Closer to the juncture of hallway and parlor. Cass strained to parse visual details from the gloom.

Her eyes snapped wide. Ice water flooded her veins.

Belmar's lifeless body lay intwined within the demon worm's powerful coils, his arms and one leg cocked wildly at the joints as she continued to squeeze and manipulate her meal. The man's glazed eyes bulged to stare back at her, equally shocked by this predicament. The snake had swallowed Belmar's right leg to the thigh before its efforts stalled at the man's crotch.

As she watched, the monster began choking itself backward to surrender the attempt. Unblinking and fixed, Cass saw her own shadow reflected in the serpent's dead eyes. That black marble gaze appeared to be both resolved and committed.

Cass thought the bitch had taken the same measure of their shared situation to draw the same conclusion. A petite old lady seemed a more certain fit than a fully grown man. Both anticipated the next – and only – item left on demon worm's menu.

Now Cat Lady sized the wider context of her predicament. During the night, she thought the beast had made several frustrated attempts to swallow her dead lover. Though this might be the last, Cass hoped the demon worm could not easily disengage from its aborted meal. Its jaws and throat worked tortuously to back its body down Belmar's mucous-smeared leg, so she guessed the delay might provide a half-hour headstart. Fifteen minutes, at least.

Next, she visually searched for means of survival. Sam's discarded wallet and keyring lay atop an end table perched next to the sofa – the same sofa where Belmar vomited forth from the belly of the beast.

Standing deathly still, she turned only her head. Sam's pistol remained on her kitchen table where Belmar had foolishly left it. Several of the monster's coils looped there, too close to chance.

Instead, her shotgun leaned next to her shattered front door. This, in turn, stood propped open in a sharp slant, where a hole in her rusted screen proved the snake's point of entry.

It had crawled silently through the house to take Belmar while he slept. Speaking aloud to the demon worm, Cassie chided, "Your eyes got too big for your stomach. Stupid."

Given the absence of a human-shaped lump in its tube-like body, Cass decided the serpent had not eaten Sam either. She wondered if it had tried and failed, as with Belmar. The Bobs, too. Maybe.

"Nobody will blame you for barfing one or the other, or all of them." Cass vowed she would not be the serpent's fifth attempt.

On a spring-loaded bolt, she darted across the room, snatched her shotgun and Sam's keyring, flung her front door aside and then kicked open her screen. Charging across her porch to a sound of drumbeat footsteps, Cass immediately plunged into the temporary moat that surrounded her homestead. Though she could not waste time to hesitate, neither could she suppress the horrified scream that breeched her throat.

Scores of two-foot long serpents scattered from the shelter of her home's riotous hedge, so they seemed bound to race her escape. Cassie set her jaw, determined to win.

Though she consciously told herself that she need not fear the younglings given their size, Cass kept the shotgun lifted high above her wading waist. Splaying her arms wide, she alternately pointed her weapon at the nearest interloper, if only to make herself feel better about being unable to see her feet.

Every fifth step or so, she glanced backwards over her shoulder to check the demon worm's progress. She thought this interval might be short enough to catch the monster slithering into the water behind her, while also focusing minimal attention to her escape.

Pondering a short future that included the feel of a giant porker sliding between her ankles, Cass screamed from a sense of dread, disgust and rage. "I should have set the house on fire!"

Five minutes and perhaps a hundred slow, sloshing strides transpired. The serpent apparently remained hung-up on Belmar's chilled corpse.

Halfway to the road, she neared a final gentle arc in the limestone ridge that supported her overgrown and now drowned driveway. Glancing back again, she thought she saw movement among the dull shadows that filled her parlor.

As the sun continued to rise, darkness retreated and her perspective improved. Twenty more struggling strides passed. No sign of pursuit.

Five more waddling paces placed her at the verge of the bend, the point where she could no longer maintain direct line of sight to her porch. When her head snapped backwards for the last time, she gasped to see a long, thick, green-black cable curving through her threshold, across her porch, down its steps, and then into the water.

Already, the demon worm swam for her, its enormous length lending it a visible lead. As seen through her bulging eyeballs, its head seemed to be only feet away, though the true distance stretched closer to one-hundred yards.

"Oh, shit!" *She swims fast!*

Cass wished she could rise like Jesus to run on water. No mortal ever made a more convincing attempt.

Minutes later, gasping and panting, she struggled out of flooded sawgrass and onto the road. Her legs ached. Her lungs burned. Her heart kneaded her breast with terrible ferocity.

Though she longed to collapse and rest, instinct drove her. That voice of warning screamed RUN!

Glancing southbound along the blacktop, she saw how the road dipped and rose repeatedly through inundated swamp. Having weathered many violent storms there, she knew the water would stand to her chin in some places should she choose to go that way.

Northbound, the two-lane traced the same submerged ridge of limestone that supported the homesteads scattered along its length. In that direction, the lanes climbed ever so slightly toward Bailey's store. No overflow would stand deeper than her knees.

At the crossroads, she would have options. Bailey's phone might be functional.

Its jingle reminded her of Sam's keyring, which dangled from the fingers of her left hand. Jogging down the road toward the Dell homeplace, she kept a cautious eye on both sides of her advance.

She wondered where Sam had gone. She knew the snake was coming in a rush. Glancing backwards, as always, she watched for its approach.

When it remained hidden even after she had reached the entrance to Sam's shack, Cassie's worries changed direction. Slowing to keep the last few feet of storm-ravaged foliage between her and Sam's windows, she hissed, "That evil witch is stalking me from the swamp."

A cloister of cypress boughs crossed over the road along its entire length. Rolling eyes upward, she noted a close dangle of Spanish-moss and parasitic creepers. Any one of those twisted roots might be *her*.

She could attack from anywhere. "Wicked bitch!"

Sam's place appeared to be deserted. Its windows remained dark despite the gloom of dawn, but she expected him to be sleeping through last night's drunk. At any rate, her slow, inch-wise approach revealed an empty porch. A shuttered front door. His truck sat parked beside his house.

Selecting the most likely candidate, Cass gripped the keys between the fingers of her fist, intending to use them like a stabbing weapon if she must. Holding her shotgun at a sharp, ready cant – and stooping for some reason – she started along Sam's short driveway toward his vehicle.

She must wade runoff to her ankles, but this would not prove an impediment to the truck. Cass wondered how deep the draft must be for a big porker to ambush her with its looped coils.

She shuddered. She continued wading as quietly as possible, having no better option. Inside Sam's truck, she could drive to Bailey's place in five minutes. Fifteen minutes more would deliver her into town.

Ducking behind its crumpled rear fender, Cass allowed only the top of her head and watchful eyes to linger above its shelter. Duck-waddling through the soup, she moved to its passenger side door, this being the one facing away from Sam's house.

Through its windshield, she could see he left it unlocked. Easier and easier.

Clamping its keys between her teeth, Cass tried the truck's latch with her left hand. It popped. The door thumped open. Its rusted hatch ground on its hinges as she pulled it wide.

Sam's first barrage started her heart with a painful leap, so only a sharp gasp prevented it from bursting out of her throat. Instantly, she realized how she had foolishly put herself in the same position that she had, herself, hoped to use against Sam. Given Florida's laws, he could now legally shoot her for a looter. Probably using his daddy's big bore semi-automatic pistol.

Fifteen slugs lanced through the darkened windows of his home. Glass shattered all around her ducking head to make a diamond-studded shower of slanted morning sunshine. Huge, ragged holes punched through the pickup's steel doors and quarter-panels. All its windshields burst, one after another.

Cass had already bolted for the cover of the roadway, where it stretched northward behind the overgrown greenery that suffocated the Dell holler. As her ears recovered from an initial assault of gunfire, she heard Sam raging drunkenly from inside his shack. He promised her all manner of mischief, and she knew he must be reloading.

Once she cleared his line of sight, she threw his keys into the swamp as far as her slender arm would allow. Then, not knowing if Sam could still start the truck behind her, Cat Lady Cassie started running along the center stripe, bound for the dubious sanctuary of Bailey's tumbledown store. Sprung prey, she would not stop running for seven uninterrupted miles.

SEGMENT 23

All southern men worth their weight will carry a blade of some kind on their person. This might be a humble penknife reserved for the grooming of cuticles and the like, or it might be a more substantial belt-clasped, fixed-blade variety. Forever being a man in the middle, Sam wore a modest utility tool on his belt for so long that it had worn a custom groove there. Most days, he forgot about it.

Wrapped in three full loops of ravenous green anaconda, his pistol lost to the first blows of ambush, Sam ultimately remembered this forgotten salvation. Sucking what he knew to be his last living breath, he held this wind in a way that he had never held any other – like a stoppered cork threatening to burst explosively.

The demon worm had strangled thousands of animals, so she understood Sam's response as a last stand prior to unconsciousness and death. She must simply press this final gasp from her prey's lungs, and then she could feed.

His life measured in the numb movements of fingers, hand and arm, Sam fumbled the tool's main blade open using an expert, one-fisted draw. Rotating it delicately through tingling fingers tinting blue, he next oriented it in his grip, intending to stab backward over his left shoulder, where he believed her head to dangle.

A sound of breaking bones stroked the hollow spaces of his compressed torso. Perhaps a half-dozen ribs fractured, one after another, but he somehow held his last breath.

Stubbornly, he thought of Cassie, and he knew he could never allow the matters between them to end so easily for her. As though provoked by thoughts of a real, actual devil, the demon worm struck savagely to bite down atop Sam's balding head.

Its patient breath hissed through a thick tracheal tube that pressed against his cheek. Her teeth started a ratchet slide over his immobile body, so its jaws worked wider and wider around his ears, chewing inexorably toward his shoulder. Sam smelled and tasted the foul, rotten-fish odor of its gulping maw. Everything inside the animal felt cold and slimy and impossibly hard.

Phosgene stars swarmed his dimming vision. Dark clouds pooled and swirled at the periphery of his gaze. As a bad dream, he watched one tingling arm rising slowly – too slowly – its crushed upper length starved of oxygen.

Clamping his tongue to the roof of his mouth and screwing his jaws together, tooth-to-tooth, Sam strained powerfully. His head swelled to make a purple mask of his face. That last breath verged at the top of his choking throat. Vision narrowed. Thoughts slowed.

Making certain of his aim, since it might be his last living act, Sam drove his knife savagely backwards. This being the sort of blade with a deeply serrated aft edge, its blunt point punched through the underside of the snake's massive mouth. There, it hung on its serrations, caught in the cartilage and musculature that powered the base of its tongue.

Sam never knew snakes could scream. He distinctly heard this sound whistle through the constrictor's distended breathing tube as it instantly reacted to his assault.

Having only begun to feed, she quickly disengaged her attempt to devour him whole, even as the intensity of her crush also relaxed. The loose ends of her massive body thrashed unhappily, while her head loomed wide and away from its prey, her jaws working furiously to dislodge the spike in her gullet.

Moments before blackout, Sam felt this release. Without issuing conscious thoughts directing it to do so, he felt his body thrash free of her crushing embrace, his raw, jerking motions powered by the force of sheer, autonomous instinct.

By the time sufficient circulation returned to his brain to restart his sense of self-awareness, Sam found himself sloshing through the shallows that already overflowed Cassie's storm-racked holler. Half-drunk and all-terrified, he somehow made his way home, where he collapsed into bed fully clothed, mud-splattered, and still slathered in the anaconda's digestive-slime. His shattered ribs ached with each wheeze. Otherwise, upon awakening the next morning, he might have dismissed the entire experience for an unsettling nightmare.

Segment 23

SEGMENT 24

During summer storms, Bailey roomed above his humble shop, feeling no need to evacuate and every need to protect his business from looters. His great-grandfather, his grandfather and his own father had served the same duty down through so many generations of the Matchlock family. Folks invariably needed unexpected sundries after nature's havoc, and they tended to resolve those needs one way or another. So, his family had learned to make the sale, rather than the repair.

Having weathered countless smaller tempests and some larger, Bailey had no cause to fear wind, rain or flood. The crossroads purposefully took advantage of underlying limestone deposits, which naturally lifted most of the roadway a scant foot or so above the swamp's two-hundred-year flood stage.

Long before any government paved a lane there, Bailey's great-grandfather had built the first Matchlock family store on the intersection's northeast corner, now just across the diagonal. A shuttered automotive service shop stood there today – also a Matchlock family concern.

Its proprietor, Cousin Kimmy, preferred to be at home with her family during foul weather. As did Cousin Wilburn, proprietor of the café that occupied the crossroads' southeast corner, and Cousin Jessup, the ne'er-do-well of the clan and self-appointed 'general-manager' of the 'Apparel Mart', which had devolved into a kind of flea-market under Jessup's drug-addled management.

Bailey sighed leadenly. He sat atop his stool.

From this vantage, he alternated his attention between the rain-pelted landscape as seen through his windows, and monotonous storm reports, which he watched on a small television monitor that hung overhead and to one side of a dangling cigarette rack. Alongside this televised feed of increasingly strident forecasts, several other monitors played split-screen scans of each shop's security cameras. As a family should do, each Matchlock watched over every other.

Never mind wind, lightning and flood, hard experience taught Bailey that the storm's greatest threat invariably stalked about on two, desperate legs. Thinking this dark thought, Bailey crossed his arms over another bored sigh. His gaze dropped to the cabinets underneath his countertop. Among the various sundries that law required him to keep hidden until purchase, he once more registered the presence of his stumpy shotgun, its barrel and stock cut to the sheerest limits allowed by law.

He had necessarily used the weapon more than once, and everyone thereabouts knew the Matchlocks *never* lost a dollar to a thief. Leastwise, not easily.

Mostly, though, all the locals knew the Matchlock family to be as generous as they must be to keep violence at a minimum. Everyone knew to ask before taking, since his family rarely refused credit to a neighbor. Nobody ever left Bailey's store hungry or empty-handed for want of a 'forgotten' wallet or purse.

Then again – his thoughts paused to swat a skeeter with his magazine-fan – then again, some folks are just plain bad, no matter what their neighbors might think. Like most places in a generally desperate world, much of Florida tended to be sprawled, wild and empty. Law enforcement remained sparse, and its personnel would be invariably preoccupied during a storm like this one.

Within the transpiration of such lawless hours, humankind instinctively reduced moral oversight to a matter of life-and-death. No veneer of civility ever fed a starving child. So, each citizen of the state had repeatedly voted to conserve and even expand laws of self-defense for preservation of life, limb and property.

This last bit seemed most significant, as Bailey pondered the rising gale while the store's lights flickered and failed. Again.

He fanned himself as the air-conditioning died. Moments later, a back-up generator rumbled to life. Presently, emergency circuits activated to power half the ceiling lights, his coolers, his register and his security systems. No A/C.

Unlike storms elsewhere, which often preceded or followed a precipitous plunge of temperature, tropical storms hang atop a stifling dome of hot, humid air. Should he dare to step outside, Bailey knew he would find the rainfall warm to his touch. Like tepid bathwater.

Consequently, the world steamed beneath such tempests, and relief usually followed only days – sometimes weeks – afterward. Bailey ground his teeth, prepared to sweat.

He pondered an ice-cream snack. Suffering these sweet thoughts, his harpy ex-wife screamed all the terrible obesity-related insults she had ever concocted throughout the course of their miserable marriage. So, he resisted.

Then he remembered why he had divorced that bitch in the first place. So, he dropped off his stool.

Rounding his counter, he indecisively rifled his premium ice-cream coolers to make an impossible choice.

Segment 24

So many wonderful and frosty delights! *If he must indulge, then he should only have one*, screamed his ex'. According to her shame and his guilt, he took two. A sandwich and a drumstick.

Returning to his stool, he quickly devoured the former, given its superior rate of melt. Then he hunched over to savor the latter, taking immense pleasure in each frosty bite, first through its frozen fudge topping, then through soft-serve ice-cream underneath, and finally through its chocolate cone, which revealed itself inch-upon-inch as he lovingly peeled away its paper container.

Finished, he dropped both wrappers into a trashcan heaped into a corner cabinet. Then he fussed to clean himself. Afterward, he watched curtains of rain sweep the pavement, and he felt guilty.

Moment to moment, he alternately licked tasty memories from his lips or he cursed himself for being so weak. *Nobody likes a fatso.* Then again, he thought, everybody he knew tended to be fat these days. So, inevitably, he brightened. His stomach rumbled.

Wavering later, he punished himself by extracting cash from his billfold to pay retail price for both treats. *I shouldn't rob myself twice!*

When he changed his mind again and leaned forward to retrieve his cash, a vague shadow lurched through the storm to distract him. Diverting his attention to a discerning squint, he peered into the rainswept gloom for the specter he saw huddling there. Lifting his gaze, his focus flipped through security cameras until he found an angle that confirmed his impressions.

A lone figure leaned against the wind and driving rain to struggle along the two-lane's center stripe, head down and shoulders hunched. For a moment, he gaped, wondering who might be so foolish – or desperate – to venture out afoot in such weather. Another pace or two informed him since he could not mistake that familiar shuffle.

She visited his store once per month, every month, rain or shine. He kept a special supply of feral cat bait, just for her.

"Cat Lady Cass?" he wondered aloud.

Something dangled from her hands. *A shotgun?*

"What on Earth?" as any worthy southern gent might do, given similar circumstance, Bailey dropped off his stool to fetch his own stumpy riot gun.

Since he might need to bolt the door and drop the store's steel shutters, Bailey grabbed his keys with his free hand, and then he hurried to the front windows to man locks and switches. Cass eventually emerged from the weather, her mouth moving to make a flashing black hole at the center of her face. Obviously, she shouted some form of distress, but Bailey only heard wind, rain and thunder.

"Crazy bitch," he gasped. "I couldn't hear a foghorn through a loudspeaker right now."

Peering through a gale-slanted deluge, he scanned her backtrail for pursuit. Instantly, he thought of Sam Dell and their long-simmering *situation*. Whatever it might be.

Dropping his keys into a front pocket, he next hurried to the door, ready to prop it open for her entrance. Seconds later, she burst through, slinging damp like a wet cat. Through a fading peal of thunder, he listened for the details of her lunatic rant.

"...on the telephone, you damned fool, and call for the law! The man has run amok, and no telling where that monster snake has gone!"

Segment 24

Stepping back to wrinkle his face and pinch his nose before her stink, as per tradition, Bailey fixed a dull mask to his face to drawl, "Do what?"

The safety glass of the door burst like a bubble. A neat hole appeared in both of his startled cheeks. A fine spray of blood and tissue splattered Cassie's face, which ran pink when this grim pigment mixed with the rain that soaked her being.

Feeling a sting against her neck, she instinctively reached to pinch this insult away. Examining her catch with a remote, stunned gaze, she recognized the form of a partially filled human tooth.

Lifting her attention, a perplexed Bailey mouthed soundless words at her. Rather than an expulsion of breath, his partially severed tongue delivered another, denser spray of blood. Then the man's head snapped sideways as though slapped, and his brains flew through the air and into the store's interior. Bailey dropped like the dead man that he had instantly become.

Cassie screamed and dropped, too. Scrambling backward and sideways, she moved deeper into the shop's sheltering aisles. One by one as though chasing after her desperate flight, plate-glass windows fractured around a succession of bullet holes until the collective damage sufficed to burst the entire panel. Then razor-edged shards of tempered glass lanced the air around her to scatter tiled floor with transparent knives.

She must slow to avoid skidding atop the debris. Already shredded by asphalt, her feet bled more profusely with each step.

Instinctively, she ducked. At the back of the store, the glass doors of several coolers burst into countless crystals, each eruption marking a direct line that passed

Cassie's head, tracking backwards to the blazing muzzle of a handgun, which flashed repeatedly from the gloom.

POP! POP! POP!

Someone screamed shrilly, a tiny girl frightened. Ultimately, as she rounded a rack of brain-splattered pastries, Cat Lady recognized this terrified voice as her own. She could do nothing to restrain herself, since her inner-animal had usurped control of her body and mind.

POP! POP! POP!

Lifting her hands – one hefting her shotgun – she shielded her face from flying shards as she scrambled into the store's maze of aisles. She slipped in blood or tomato-based sauce, scarcely catching her fall against a stand of sunglasses and hats before she hit the floor. There, she knew she would die, because Sam held a direct bead on the store's exposed façade, its windows all burst open.

Hidden among the gloom, he chased her darting form with the sights of his handgun. In the last moment, he drew an aim on her spine, dead-bang. He squeezed his trigger.

For all the spatter of rainfall and howl of wind, he felt more than heard the click of his pistol's hammer. *An empty chamber!*

Roaring and shaking violently, Sam snapped his pistol's magazine catch. An empty clip skipped across the blacktop and into a deep puddle as he fetched a reload from his belt. His brain operated remotely, its machinery lubricated by several quarts of rotgut alcohol, so he vaguely – yet pridefully – noted the accuracy of his aim.

He struck Bailey in the head from a range of nearly fifty yards. Twice.

As ever, Dell-luck ran best at its worst. He rarely succeeded at any productive pursuit, but he could screw-up like a professional.

Stumbling through the intersection, never mind the weather, Sam cackled, "That's some topnotch shooting, right there!"

This time, they would not charge him with a trifling offense. No, sir. This time, he shouted, "I done murder for certain sure!"

He laughed raucously, so his stumble improved until he all but collapsed to the pavement. To gather his sense of balance, Sam paused, bent over wobbly knees. His pulse throbbed delightfully. His stomach bubbled deliciously.

Had he known how freeing murder could be, he might have done the deed years – no, decades – earlier! Sure, he had sacrificed his own freedom for the thrill, but the law could no longer manage him either.

"I cut the cords, at last, Cassie!" he shouted, straightening to lift his face skyward and drink rain, his throat suddenly parched and his belly empty-dry. "No more rules! No more worries! No more nothing!"

To pontificate, Sam levered his handgun upward to take aim at the last remaining window of Bailey's storefront. POP!

Rain blurred his vision, muffled his hearing and dampened his voice. His ears rang from gunfire and endless strokes of thunder. Lightning strobed the crossroads holler, its encircling foliage alive and dancing beneath the gale.

"See? I told you I could do it! I always had the guts!" He put another round through the window as he stumped onto the store's weedy parking lot. POP! "*Always!*"

Using the back of a sodden sleeve, he cleared tears and rainwater from his eyes. He sucked snot through flared nostrils. The air stank of water and rot.

A third shot punched through the glass. POP!

This time, he stood close enough to see a small, ragged hole appear in its face. Radiating from each impact, delicate cracks spread like spider webs. Water coursed along these new fissures in the glass, so all the angles and edges sparked fiercely before each stroke of lightning. A constant rainfall spun everything into gauzy halos before Sam's drink-befuddled gaze.

Stalking through the store's twin rows of gas pumps, Sam wasted a fourth shot on the plate-glass. This time, the entire panel burst into large, razor-edged slabs, which sliced downward toward the floor with all the lethal ability of fractious guillotines.

His sloppy footfalls slid through layers of tinkling debris. When he steadied himself with an instinctive grip around one shattered frame, he scarcely felt the deep cuts inflicted there, though each bled profusely.

From the back of the store, he saw flashes before his ears registered discharges. BOOM! CHICK-CHUCK! BOOM! CHICK-CHUCK!

Cassie's pump-twenty. From a range of thirty yards, Sam felt several tiny birdshot pellets bite into his skin. Each penetration burned painfully, but he scarcely registered their impact in his drunken condition.

Mechanically, he lifted his pistol again. POP! POP! POP!

Unlike Cassie's birdshot, Sam's forty-five-caliber slugs punched big holes in everything they touched. Each round easily passed through the store's interior, stopping only after impacting the building's rear wall. Deafened by gunshots, he never heard her sharp squeals of terror, but he saw Cassie's shadow-form dart into its stockroom through a pock-marked service door.

Segment 24

Stumbling over an empty window jamb, Sam followed. Scarcely able to breathe for laughing, he pushed himself from one aisle to the next, his injured hand leaving gruesome crimson smears and palmprints along the way. These imprints dripped and splattered liberally, but he felt no pain.

"Cass, honey!" he called playfully. "Don't play hard-to-get! Not now, after all we've been through!"

A gale of hilarity forced him over bent knees, so he struggled to breathe. Straightening when he heard her working the store's backdoor, he staggered in recovery, steadying himself against various display racks that he painted bloody.

Rows of coolers lined the shop's rear wall. Closest to its bullet-pocked service door, Sam leaned against a shattered glass frame that once kept cold beer. Feeling suddenly thirsty and altogether too sober, he paused to select a bottle of malt liquor. Tucking his pistol beneath one soggy armpit, he dripped rainwater and blood and an overflow of pungent brew. It brimmed his lips to cascade his chin, its foam weaving through the bristles of his three-day beard. Like a suckling pig, he drank.

Noisily. Deeply. Breathlessly.

Through the cooler, he heard Cass struggling with the back door. Apparently, Bailey had locked it, taking the keys with him.

Listening through a gunshot-rung stupor, Sam finished his stolen bottle and dropped it to shatter on the floor at his feet. Half-turning, he confronted the stretch of Bailey's legs, which splayed into a 'V' shape that parted a widening pool of blood. He thought the man's heart must continue to beat.

Dully, he lifted his pistol. Taking aim through a rack of sandwich bread, he pointed the muzzle about where he thought Bailey's pulsing heart must lie. POP!

Those legs jumped, twitching. Nothing more.

Sam shrugged. Returning to business, he reached for the door latch. Expecting another fusillade, he stood to one side and he pulled it open with his left hand as quietly as its worn hinges would allow. His pistol dangled loosely from his right, its bore exhaling a casual smoke.

When he pulled the door wide and nothing had happened, Sam dared to lean forward so he could peer around its edge into stockroom shadows. She had extinguished the lights. *Smart girl*.

Then, nobody ever accused Cassie of stupid. Crazy, yes – every damned day – but never stupid.

In the same instant that he intended to leap through the threshold, the cooler beside him exploded. Frothing beer and ale mixed with glass, plastic and paper, all of it pelting him around a spatter of birdshot. Sam felt the sting of a hundred tiny pellets, whether of glass or lead he could not know.

Moments later, something low and sleek burst through the open doorway, moving fast. A trail of bloody footprints followed this streaking shadow, which crossed the store's counter headed toward its shattered façade.

Instinctively, Sam's right hand snapped level near his waist. POP! POP! POP!

Cass screamed and cursed him as she rounded the last aisle. There, her footfalls paused. As he realized she had left her pump-twenty in the stockroom, Sam also recalled seeing Bailey with his semi-auto twelve-gauge riot-gun.

Hoping to deter her, he lowered his barrel. POP! POP! POP! POP! POP! CLICK!

Segment 24

Sam's head swam a sea of alcohol. His eyes blinked to clear blurs of rain and sweat. For the constant crush of deluge and rage, he struggled to parse the situation and make sense of himself.

Before he could collect himself, he felt and saw rather than heard Bailey's twelve-gauge. By the time blasts cut through a dozen aisles to reach him, the buckshot had softened and expanded. Each pellet punched a ragged hole in the boxes and packages arrayed before him.

Perhaps a score of these projectiles lanced into Sam's body. He scarcely felt their impact – only the slow fade of afterburn.

Behind and all around him, countless beer bottles exploded to spray him with suds. Sam licked lips to taste brew and blood. The fingers of his left hand traced a deep gouge that arced over his skull, starting just above his right eye and terminating behind his right ear.

Strange. He felt nothing.

Shucking his pistol's spent clip, he reached for a reload, mumbling, "The power and the glory." *I am an instrument of god!*

Giggling madly, he goaded her, saying, "That's some mighty fine shooting, Cass, but you can't kill me! Not today!"

Jamming a fresh magazine into the pommel of his handgun, Sam started around the nearest rack, since the store's rear section offered superior cover. Though he stalked along with exaggerated stealth, all the smashed and shattered debris on the floor betrayed his footsteps.

Expecting another barrage of double-ought buckshot, he turned the shelf's endcap to follow his pistol back to the storefront. Since he knew she could hear his approach, he taunted her. "God wants me to do this! You and I both know why! And you can't fight god, Cass! Everybody else on the planet, maybe, but *not god!*"

As the high-pitched ring of gunshots faded from his sense of hearing, a peal of thunder reminded Sam of the storm yet raging outside. Lightning strobed the shop's half-lit interior. Another celestial cannonade followed.

He knew she could easily fade into the swamp in such weather, and he might have chased after her more urgently for this thought. Except, he lingered at the endcap of the first aisle, his bleary eyes half-focused on the monotonous sweep of rain and wind.

Glancing downward, he marked a series of bloody swirls in the pattering rainfall. Footsteps.

She had darted around the building rather than expose her back while attempting to cross the road. Sam grinned wickedly. *I've got her now!*

Any other day, Cass might evade easily into the swamp using the storm as a shroud. Not today though, because out there somewhere lurked the demon worm, and it clearly had a taste for human flesh.

Supremely arrogant in god's grace and the devil's ire, he pushed away from the shelves to cross piles of fractured glass. Sweeping blood and sweat and rain from his face with a trembling left hand, he vaguely wondered why he shook. Not from fear, but from the cold perhaps.

Grinning foolishly, half-expecting a shotgun blast to obliterate his face, Sam leaned into the rain. To his surprise, the corner of the building presented no threat.

He followed those bloody swirls, limping. Numbly, he next wondered what had gone wrong with his legs. That painless glow of immortality slipped a bit.

"The bitch shot me!" he marveled angrily.

Despite his injuries, Sam refused to question the provenance of his holy mission. As a sign, god often revealed his grace through the temperance of suffering. After all, she had hit him several times with a scattergun, pointblank and dead-bang – a stunning, if belated, realization. *Hot shit!*

Cackling wildly, he lifted his voice to the rain, and he brayed, "I'm still alive!"

Then he ducked his head to dash around the bend, fully expecting to confront his hated lover there. As soon as he rounded the corner, he fired twice into the tempest. POP! POP!

An empty walkway and parking lot greeted him with a rainswept riot. Beyond this stretch of concrete and blacktop, the encroaching swamp thrashed a crazed, storm-driven dance. Leaves and bits of debris swirled through a slanted deluge. Okeechobee's overflow streamed around the crossroads to make an island of its elevation.

Sam paused in confusion. He thought she might have quickly disappeared around the next corner, but those footprint swirls stopped abruptly. Halfway there, Cass had apparently disappeared.

Blinking dully through a cascade of tepid rainfall, Sam slowly approached the final, fading crimson swirls. His head turned the lot and the crossroads, beyond. He knew she could never run so fast with shredded feet.

Before he could resolve or surrender the mystery, something struck stars into his vision. Something hard and heavy bounced off his head, rolled over his right shoulder, and then clattered onto the pavement at his feet.

Instinctively rubbing an already abused skull, he saw Bailey's shotgun lying before the toes of his boots. Cocking a groggy head, Sam pondered its origins. Slowly, he figured the proper angle.

Lifting his gaze directly overhead, darkness engulfed him. Then a stroke of lightning flashed the half-light lurid. Everything jumped into crisp shadows and stark relief.

Sam blinked. His mouth gaped. His addled mind struggled to understand this strange vision of heaven and hell now manifest above him like an unmistakable sign from god.

Eve. Samael. Tangled together in lust. In horror.

Her eyes bulged enormously, unashamed to beg her most hated tormentor for mercy. Yet Cass could not open lips or mouth to render an audible plea because she must hold her last breath with all the tenacity of a thing dying. Her swelling countenance tinged blue with desperation. Her wiry arms struggled to free her choking throat, while her legs twitched uselessly, slinging blood like black paint.

One hand released its grip on the beast to reach for him. Soundlessly, Cass dared to part her lips. Glazed eyesight dimming, she mouthed two silent words. "Sam" and "help".

Instead, Sam holstered his weapon to clap his hands together as he danced a drunken jig. Moving away several paces to ease the strain of his neck, he mocked her with delight.

"It's the hand of god, Cass! Moving through the moment to strike the stink of you from his garden! Forever!" Sam pointed, clapped, laughed and jigged. "I bet you never thought you'd end this way, not even in your worst nightmares! Imagine the gall! A devil, eaten by a devil!"

Indeed, the demon worm had apparently snatched Cass off her feet as the woman ran beneath its dangling ambush. Half-descended from the roof, it had twisted itself around a horizontal lighting fixture to support its attack. From there, it snapped the woman off the pavement to immediately roll her thrashing body into three powerful loops of its coiled body. Cass hung halfway between roof and lot while relentless rainfall made a wet halo all around her struggling form.

Jutting above the sinuously constricting knots of its body, the serpent's massive head poised to make oral contact with its prey. This time, all its ancient senses informed the demon worm of proper fit, and it knew the woman would easily go down whole. Its lower jaws worked fluidly left to right until its bones unlocked and unhinged from its skull.

Having recently experienced this very trauma, Sam held aching ribs, but he could not stop laughing. Choking himself with it, he sat heavily backwards onto the pavement, where he rolled in the blood and the rain.

Distracted by this movement, especially when revealed by endless flashes of lightning, the serpent held its pose, ready to strike. Now its head began swaying gently in time to Sam's antics, clearly tracking him as a potential threat.

This is how he might have ended her, too, except Sam ultimately remembered his cause. Thirty-five demeaning years of emotional servitude could not be tossed aside for a good chuckle, and he could not allow the monster to steal his glory. No matter how much the prospect amused him.

Clutching guts that stirred with an oddly ominous sensation, Sam dragged himself to his feet. First, he considered using his pistol. Next, he decided to use Bailey's shotgun instead.

This, he retrieved from the pavement. Awaiting a stroke of lightning, he half-jacked its slide to confirm the presence of a live round in its chamber. Lifting this overhead, his uncertain stupor made a blur of his target, never mind the minimal range. Buckshot could make a big hole there – maybe too big.

Sam lowered the weapon. He watched Cassie's eyes glaze over, moment to moment. Perhaps half-a-minute remained of her last gasp.

Chuckling, he determined to strangle the woman himself. An errant shotgun blast would not deliver the same sense of satisfaction.

So, he safed the weapon and turned it around in his grasp. Using this like a bat, he rose to tiptoes, and then he struck the serpent's head a direct and solid blow. It dodged away, of course, being so much quicker than the man – and considerably less intoxicated.

Yet it also registered his attack. Sensing unconsciousness in its prey, the demon worm relaxed its grip to drop the woman onto the ground.

There, it would feed in time. First, it must resolve this unexpected challenge to its meal.

As Sam continued to swing at the beast, alternately laughing and praising god, the demon worm reset its coils to renew its assault. When the woman toppled from its slackened loops, the man immediately dropped his weapon to fetch her lifeless body.

Dragging this backward and, so, further into the parking lot, Sam blubbered, "No, no, no, no! Don't die, Cass! Stay alive, so I can kill you!"

Pausing a safe distance from Bailey's ruined store, Sam blew several breaths into Cassie's gaping, rain-filled mouth. His former lover coughed, sputtering. Her pain-wracked body seized violently as her brain reconnected to its vital supply of oxygen.

She awakened beneath the full moon of Sam's overhanging face, his features contorted by madness and brilliant flashes of lightning. Struggling to understand her

Segment 24

condition, she last remembered awakening to an empty bed, thinking Sam had returned to kill her at last.

Epileptic and nonsensical, her limbs thrashed wildly. Instinctively, her fingers and toes sought for some purchase on reality, however tenuous.

Amid the confusion, her grip fell on a familiar object. In the same moment, her eyes snapped wide, their focus extending beyond the hateful mask of Sam's raging countenance.

Behind his back, the demon worm loomed, its distended jaws gaping wide and its black eyes fixed forward, determined to finish its meal. Its pink tongue curled forth, flicked up and down, and then retracted. Its massive head swayed back and forth, left and right, up and down, clearly confused by the human struggle that sprawled beneath it.

Ultimately, it decided. It struck.

Cass rolled away through parking lot puddles with Sam's pistol held firmly in her right hand. Behind her, the demon worm balled itself around Sam's torso while its maw gaped, hissing.

With astonishing speed and expertise, it added the bulk of its mass to the tangle, somehow managing to hold its head high despite violent resistance. Seconds later, only the man's fingers, feet and head protruded from its powerful coils.

Each pulse drew it tighter. Sam groaned miserably. Though he longed to laugh because fate seemed so damned funny, he thought better. Instead, he determined to preserve his last breath. For her.

Through the collapsing vision of fading eyesight, he watched Cass scramble backward until she could plant her feet. Then she rose, trembling but whole. His daddy's pistol dangled from her right fist, but she refused to save him with it.

His eyes rolled painfully. *No surprise.*

Disgusted, she let rainfall purge the serpent's stink from her body while she watched Sam suffer and die. This time, the last time.

Because his lips moved, she listened. *Why not?* Whether by pistol or serpent, he would never torment her again.

Fixing her shadow-bound form in his dimming gaze, Sam judiciously spent his last breath, croaking each syllable to be clear. He said, "I never told... about the bullet... in your parlor ceiling."

Then he died. She watched a familiar fade dim his eyes, and she knew. *Gone forever.*

Through a sly smirk, she purred. "Good-boy."

Segment 24

Segment 24

SEGMENT 25

    Trailing bloody footprint swirls, Cass limped sidelong toward the storefront where Bailey's pudgy body stiffened and cooled. She kept her eyes steadily fixed on the demon worm, if only to time its movements against her own.

    Having stifled Sam's earthly struggles, the serpent immediately began to uncoil itself from its latest kill, which it already knew to be too large for consumption. While it worked, its jaws twisted back and forth again until its bones snapped back into place. Through all, its beady black eyes sparkled ravenously and its deadly attention never wavered from Cassie's limping retreat.

    Measuring her future in heartbeats, Cass disappeared around the corner. Moments later, she reappeared wearing a dead man's shoes. Then she quickly disappeared into the storm, gimping northbound along the two-lane's inundated center stripe as fast as shredded feet would allow.

    Behind her fleeing back, its graceful serpentine as patient as a rising flood, her demon worm followed...

IF YOU ENJOYED THIS STORY, PLEASE REWARD THE AUTHOR WITH A POSITIVE VOTE AND REVIEW. YOUR INPUT MAKES ALL THE DIFFERENCE!

END